D0963191

Mandie Mysteries

———

Mandie's Cookbook

MANDIE

AND THE
CHEROKEE LEGEND

Lois Gladys Leppard

BETHANY HOUSE PUBLISHERS

MINNEAPOLIS, MINNESOTA 55438

Library of Congress Catalog Card Number 83-70894

ISBN 0-87123-321-5

Published by Bethany House Publishers
A Division of Bethany Fellowship, Inc.
6820 Auto Club Road, Minneapolis, Minnesota 55438

Printed in the United States of America

For My Brother and My Sisters,

James Matthew Leppard,
Margaret Louise Leppard Langer,
Sibyl Belle Leppard Langford,

In Memory of Our Childhood Joys and Sorrows.

About the Author

LOIS GLADYS LEPPARD has been a Federal Civil Service employee in various countries around the world. She makes her home in Greenville, South Carolina.

The stories of her own mother's childhood are the basis for many of the incidents incorporated in this series.

Table of Contents

MANDIE'S TRAVELS

Cave

Deep Creek

○ Uncle Ned's House

Little Tennessee River

Cherokee Hospital ○

Bryson City ○

Almond Station ○

Tomahawk Trail

Bird-town

Cherokee Reservation

Council House ○

Asheville ○

Joe's House ○

Buckner Branch

Little Tennessee River

Charley Gap ○

Tuckasegee River

Nantahala River

Wiggins Creek

Tomahawk Trail

Hightower Gap

Ruby Mine ○

Franklin ○

North Carolina

Georgia

South Carolina

To Charleston

Chapter 1 / Mandie and the Panther

Mandie sat with her feet dangling in the cool water of the Tuckasegee River. Her white kitten, Snowball, played at the edge of the rocks. It was a hot day for the North Carolina mountains and Mandie was tired. Slipping away from the others, she had hastily pulled off her shoes and stockings, thrown her bonnet on a nearby bush, and run down the bank to the river.

She had left her fine clothes at home and traveled in calico. Mandie and her new family were on their way to visit her Cherokee kinpeople, none of whom she had ever seen. She was wondering if the Cherokees would like her. After all, she was only one-fourth Cherokee herself, and not only that, she didn't even look like an Indian with her long blonde hair and bright blue eyes.

It was so important to Mandie that the Cherokees like her, because they were her father's people, and her dear father was now in heaven.

A faint sound behind Mandie startled her, bringing her out of her reverie. She was so frightened, it took all her willpower to turn her head to see what it was. To her horror, directly behind her the beady eyes of a panther watched as it crouched menacingly in a chestnut tree, ready to spring. She froze, her heartbeat pulsating wildly in her throat as she gasped in fright. The others were all up at the wagon on the road. There was no one to help her. No one, that is, but God. *Please, dear God, make the panther go away*, she silently prayed, her eyes never leaving the animal. She knew she shouldn't have slipped away by herself. The beady eyes still watched her.

Then out of the corner of her eye, she caught a glimpse of a young Indian boy standing in the nearby bushes. He looked at her, then at the panther, then turned to walk away.

"Help me! Please!" she whispered hoarsely.

The boy glanced back but continued on his way. Never in her life had Mandie hated anyone as she did that boy right then.

Suddenly, from another direction, an arrow winged through the air striking the beast in the tree. Mandie held her breath—appearing through the trees was Uncle Ned! The thrill of relief flooded her body.

"Don't move, Papoose!" the old Indian cautioned, as he quickly moved forward.

The panther, severely wounded, loosened its grip and fell from the tree. Mandie scrambled up the bank, her white kitten leaping after her.

"Uncle Ned! Where did you come from?" she asked as she paused to put on her shoes and stockings over her wet feet.

"Papoose take too long to get to Cherokee house. I come see why," he replied, turning the panther over. "Go back to wagon, now. I come soon. Wait there."

The girl snatched her bonnet from the bush where she had left it, calling back as she ran up the hill, "Hurry,

Uncle Ned. We'll wait for you."

She hurried through the trees, and as she caught sight of the others at the wagon on the road, she called out, "Mother! Uncle John! Uncle Ned is here!"

Her mother and Uncle John, standing under the shade of the trees, turned to look at her. Her friend, Joe, came from around the wagon.

"Where, Mandie?" asked Uncle John.

"Down there—down at the river," she replied, pointing back at the way she had come. "Oh, it was awful! I was washing my feet and this panther was up in the tree getting ready to attack me when all of a sudden Uncle Ned came out of the woods and shot him with one of his arrows!"

The other three looked at one another, startled.

"Slow down, Amanda," her mother told her. "You're out of breath."

"Oh, and there was this Indian boy standing there in the woods, but he wouldn't help me at all; and he saw the panther, too," she continued. "He just turned around and walked away, leaving me there helpless and alone."

Uncle John lifted a rifle from the wagon and started down the hill. "Let me go see what Uncle Ned is doing. He might need some help."

"Guess I'll go, too," called Joe, hurrying after John.

"Amanda, dear, please don't *ever* go off alone like that again," her mother pleaded. "Something awful could have happened to you."

"I'm sorry, Mother," Mandie said soberly, putting her arm around her mother's waist. "But it was so hot I just had to wash my feet to cool off a little. It has been such a long journey all the way from Franklin. Wonder how much farther we have to go?"

"I know, I know," her mother replied, stroking the blonde curls. "We are all hot and tired. It shouldn't be much farther. Uncle Ned will know."

When the men came up the hill with Joe, Mandie ran to meet them. She hugged the old Indian. "You always come just in time, Uncle Ned."

"I promise Jim Shaw I see after Papoose when he go to happy hunting ground," the old Indian reminded her.

"I know, Uncle Ned, but now that I have found my real mother and she has married my Uncle John, you don't have to worry about me," the girl replied.

"May be fine, but I promise. I keep promise. Even when Papoose get to be squaw and marry Joe here, I keep promise," he told her, with a twinkle in his eyes.

Joe blushed and kicked at the stones under his feet. He intended to marry Mandie when they grew up, but he certainly didn't want people talking about it. He stole a quick glance at Mandie. She was looking at him.

"I'm glad, Uncle Ned. If you had not come along when you did, I don't know what might have happened to me. I probably wouldn't be here to tell about it," Mandie admitted. "Did you see that Indian boy in the woods there? He just looked at me, and then at the panther and walked away."

The old man turned quickly toward her, his eyes squinting. "I no see Indian boy. Where he go?"

"I don't know. He just disappeared into the woods," she replied.

The old man tightened his lips and murmured, "Mmm."

"All right, let's get going," Uncle John said, changing the mood. "We want to get to Uncle Ned's house before sundown."

The road they traveled on ran parallel to the Tuckase-gee River for many miles. After a while Uncle John turned the wagon onto an old wooden bridge and crossed to the other side, traveling upward along the banks of Deep Creek.

"Oh, how I'd love to get into that water!" Mandie exclaimed, as she peered at its clear, shallow stillness.

Joe leaned out to look. "There're enough rocks to walk plumb through it."

"Won't be long now," Uncle John called back to them from his seat at the front.

And it wasn't long before cornfields started showing up along the way. Here and there tobacco was growing. At one place a hog ran grunting across the road in front of the wagon, causing the horses to buck and snort. There was an odor of food cooking, and as they came around a sharp bend in the road, a settlement of log cabins came into view. Mandie and Joe became excited.

"Looks like we're here!" exclaimed Joe.

"I can't wait to meet all my kinpeople!" Mandie cried.

"Just better not be any boys among them casting their eyes on you," Joe warned.

Mandie's mouth dropped. "I do believe you have a jealous streak in you, Joe Woodard."

"Remember, you promised. I get your father's house back from that woman he was married to, and you'll marry me!" Joe reminded her.

"Oh, Joe, it'll be years and years before you'll be old enough," Mandie replied.

"Not so long. I'm past thirteen already."

They were slowing down in front of the largest cabin in the group. There was a barn at the rear and horses could be seen behind a split-rail fence. The house looked very similar to the one in which Mandie had lived with her father. It was made of logs chinked together, with a huge rock chimney at one end. The door stood open, and they could smell the strong odor of food cooking.

"This is where Uncle Ned lives," Uncle John called back to the two young ones. He stopped the wagon by the barn and helped Elizabeth down as Uncle Ned took the reins to unhitch the horses. Mandie and Joe jumped down and looked around. There, standing across the road, was the Indian boy she had seen in the woods.

"Uncle Ned, look! There's the boy I saw in the woods!" she called, pointing to the boy.

Uncle Ned turned to look. "Oh, that Tsa'ni. He go to school. He not good Indian. I not know why he not kill panther."

An Indian squaw with a red kerchief tied around her head appeared at the door of the cabin. Mandie ran to hug her.

"Morning Star! I'm so glad to see you!" she squealed.

The old Indian woman grunted and held her tightly.

"She can't speak English, but she understands what we say pretty well," Uncle John told Mandie.

"I know. She came with Uncle Ned when he brought me to your house in Franklin," she replied. "But how did you know?"

Uncle John winked and smiled. "I stayed here at Deep Creek with the Cherokees while you were at my house hunting for my will, remember?"

"Oh, yes, of course," she laughed.

Uncle Ned and Morning Star motioned for them to come inside the log cabin. Mandie set Snowball down and looked around. It was very similar to her father's house in Charley Gap. There was a huge rock fireplace with the kettles hanging in it. A homemade table nearby was draped with a cloth, and when Morning Star removed the cloth, Mandie saw that the table was set and supper was ready and waiting.

At the far end of the room were several beds built into the wall and covered with cornshuck mattresses. Curtains hanging between them could be pulled around each one. Over in the other corner was a spinning wheel and a loom. And against the wall was a ladder going upstairs where Mandie knew there would be more beds.

"Food sure smells good!" Joe exclaimed.

Uncle Ned was speaking Cherokee to Morning Star, explaining who Mandie's mother was. All the Cherokees had known her father and now Morning Star embraced her mother. With tears in her eyes, Elizabeth smiled at the old woman.

In his Indian fashion, Uncle Ned tried to make the white people feel welcome. "Wash! Eat!" he told them, pointing to a washpan on a shelf. A clean towel was hanging on a nail beside it. A bucketful of fresh drinking water was also nearby with a gourd dipper hanging on a nail over it. Ned was a full-blooded Indian, but he knew how the white people lived.

"Save food for Snowball," Uncle Ned told Mandie, handing her a pan from the shelf. She understood they were to save the scraps from their plates for the kitten.

A beautiful young Indian girl about Mandie's age came through the open door. She was wearing a long, full skirt with a ruffled blouse; multicolored beads hung from her slender neck. Her long, black hair was held back by a red ribbon. Moving silently in her soft moccasins, she smiled as she came forward.

Uncle Ned put his arm around the girl. "This my

son's papoose. She Sallie," he told the others.

"Hello, Sallie, I'm Amanda Shaw—Mandie for short,"
Mandie greeted her. "This is my mother, Elizabeth Shaw;
my stepfather, who is also my uncle, John Shaw; and my
friend, Joe Woodard, the doctor's son."

"Welcome," Sallie replied. "I know John Shaw. We
are so excited to have you all visit us." Her speech indi-
cated she was well educated.

Elizabeth took her small brown hand in hers. "Sallie,
we are so happy to be here."

"Yes, we are, Sallie," John Shaw added.

Joe stole a glance, admiring her dark beauty, and
then put in his greeting. "Sallie, we love your grandfather,
Uncle Ned."

Morning Star spoke quietly to Uncle Ned and he an-
nounced loud and clear, "We eat now! Eat! Sit! Sit!"

The adults gathered at one side of the table and were
soon deep in conversation. Mandie found a place on the
other side between Joe and Sallie. Morning Star took the
plates to the kettles over the fire, filled them, and brought
them back to the table. Uncle Ned passed them around.

"Give thanks, John Shaw," Uncle Ned spoke again,
as Morning Star sat down.

They all bowed their heads as Uncle John raised his
voice in thanks. "We give thanks to thee, O Father, that
we are all together, and for the wonderful food prepared
for this meal. Bless this house and the people that dwell
here. Amen."

"Guess we can eat now," Joe remarked.

"Yes," Sallie told him and then turning to Mandie,
she said, "I was very sorry to hear about your father. I remember Jim Shaw. He used to visit us now and then."

Mandie was surprised. "You knew my father! Well,

yes, I suppose you did. Uncle Ned said my father used to come to visit his people here."

"All the Cherokees loved Jim Shaw. He was a good man," the Indian girl said. "My father is dead also. I live here with my grandfather and my grandmother."

"And I have known your grandfather all my life. At least, ever since I can remember. He always came to sell the baskets the Cherokees made. And I never even knew I was part Cherokee until Uncle Ned told me, after my father went to heaven. My grandmother was Talitha Pindar, a full-blooded Cherokee," Mandie told her.

"I know. The Cherokees all know who you are," Sallie said. "Eat. It is owl stew. It is very good."

Joe, who was listening to their conversation, almost choked as he stuttered, "Owl—st-stew?"

"Yes, it is something special Morning Star makes."

Mandie swallowed hard and lowered her spoon into the delicious-smelling bowl of stew in front of her. She sipped it, blinked her eyes, and smiled. "It *is* very good." Then she dug in, thinking, *This is what the Cherokees eat and I am part Cherokee.*

Joe had to follow suit. There was no way he could let a girl outdo him. Then he also smiled and said, "Say, we'll have to get Morning Star's recipe for this to take back home." He reached for a piece of beanbread and washed it all down with a huge swallow of coffee.

"I suppose you know Tsa'ni?" Mandie asked Sallie.

"Of course. He lives right down the road. He is the grandson of your father's uncle, Wirt Pindar, who lives in Bird-town," the Indian girl told her.

"Now, let me think that one out. In other words, he is my great uncle Wirt Pindar's grandson? That would make him my cousin!"

"Yes. He goes to school and is very intelligent, but has no common sense about him," Sallie said. "He—he thinks too much."

"I see. Well, I guess he was thinking too much, or something, today, when he left me with a panther staring at me." Mandie told her about the incident by the river.

"You might as well know. He does not like white people," Sallie said. "The English for his name is John, but he refuses to use it and goes by his Cherokee name. Most of us are called by our English names."

"He doesn't like white people? Why?" Mandie wanted to know.

"Because the white people destroyed our nation and took our people's land and homes and forced them to move away," Sallie said.

"I know that was wrong, terribly wrong, but that was a long time back in history. The white people living today had nothing to do with it," Mandie protested. "Besides, it was my grandfather who rescued my grandmother and her people."

Joe leaned forward. "Oh, Sallie, you've got to come to Franklin and see Mandie's Uncle John's house. It's complete with tunnels and hidden rooms, and all. Her grandfather had all this done to hide the Cherokees who didn't want to leave that area."

"I must see it, then," agreed Sallie. "It sounds very interesting. Is that where you live now, Mandie?"

"Yes, since my father died," she replied. "Uncle Ned helped me get to Uncle John's house. And then Uncle John found my real mother, and here we are!"

"Most of your kinpeople live in Bird-town," Sallie said.

"That's what Uncle Ned said. After we visit with you a day or two, we'll be going over there. Is it far to Bird-town?"

"No, but by wagon you have to follow the road instead of cutting through the woods and that makes it longer. Probably two, three hours."

The grown-ups were getting up from the table.

"You men go sit and visit and you young ones go along with Sallie outside. I will help Morning Star clear the table," Elizabeth volunteered.

"I have to feed Snowball first," Mandie told her, and holding out the pan Uncle Ned had given her, she waited for her mother to fill it with food left on the plates, which was very little, except for Joe's. He had not eaten all the owl stew, she noticed. She took the pan over to the hearth and the kitten purred contentedly as he hastily ate the food.

"He was hungry!" Sallie laughed.

"Come on. He'll follow us outside after he finishes," Mandie told her.

"Yeh, you sure can't lose that cat. He follows you like a shadow," Joe said as they went out into the yard.

Tsa'ni was sitting on a log under a hickory nut tree nearby. Sallie steered them in his direction. He stared at them silently as the group approached. Mandie could sense hate emanating from his dark eyes.

"Tsa'ni, this is your cousin, Mandie Shaw, and her friend, Joe Woodard," Sallie told him.

The boy looked from one to another and merely nodded his head without saying a word.

Mandie did not like the boy, but she knew she must at least speak to him because he was her cousin. She could still visualize the panther sitting in the tree and Tsa'ni walking away.

"Hello, Tsa'ni. Could we sit with you?" she ventured.

He immediately moved all the way down to the end of the long log.

"Sit. The log belongs to Sallie's grandfather. It is not mine," he told them.

They sat down, Mandie next to Tsa'ni.

"Mandie lived at Charley Gap with her father before he died," the Indian girl told him.

"Charley Gap? Tsali, our great warrior, whom you white people call Charley, lived in a cave near here before you white people killed him," Tsa'ni said.

"He did? I know the story of Charley, how he fought with the soldiers during the removal and killed one—" Mandie told him.

Tsa'ni interrupted, "—and how your soldiers forced Cherokee prisoners to shoot him down when he surrendered. You killed his brother and his two sons."

"I didn't kill anyone, Tsa'ni. Let's get this straight. What we are talking about was long ago in history—" Mandie's voice raised.

"I know, I know," he interrupted again.

"That was something I was not responsible for, nor my family," continued Mandie. "You can't live in the past, and you can't change history. As far as that goes, the Yankees killed my grandfather during the War of Northern Aggression, but I don't hold a grudge against the people living in the North now. They had nothing to do with it."

"Cherokee blood must be thicker than white blood then," Tsa'ni said.

"Well, just remember my grandmother was a full-blooded Cherokee," Mandie reminded him.

Joe, anxious to smooth the feelings between the two, spoke up, "Could we go see this cave, Tsa'ni?"

The Indian boy hesitated a moment, looking at Mandie. "Sure. It is not far. I will take you there tomorrow, all of you."

Mandie spoke up. "I'd really like to see it, Tsa'ni."

"I will go with you," Sallie added.

The sky was almost completely dark and the air was becoming much cooler. Snowball came bouncing across the yard and jumped into Mandie's lap.

"And so will Snowball," Mandie laughed, snuggling the kitten on her shoulder.

Tomorrow would be a day long to be remembered.

Chapter 2 / Lost in the Cave

Mandie awoke the next morning to the sound of a rooster crowing, and she had to think for a minute before she knew where she was. Sallie was asleep on the corn-shuck mattress next to her, and she knew Joe was sleeping on the other side of the rough hand-sawed wall dividing the room. She pulled the long cotton nightgown over her head and quickly reached for her dress hanging on a nail. Today was not a day to be wasted sleeping. She was in Uncle Ned's house, among the *Cherokees*!

The Indian girl looked up at her and smiled.

"You are in a hurry," she said.

"Yes, I don't have a minute to spare. I want to enjoy everything I can about our visit," Mandie replied.

From beyond the wall, Joe called to them, "Right. We gotta get going so we can go with Tsa'ni to the cave. Remember?"

"Of course," Mandie agreed.

"I smell coffee. Someone else is already up," the Indian girl commented as she, too, pulled on her skirt and blouse.

23

The three hurried down the ladder and found Uncle Ned, Uncle John, and Elizabeth sitting at the table. Morning Star was tending a pot over the fire.

"Good morning," Mandie called, as she came down the ladder.

"Come, eat," Uncle Ned said as they lined up at the washpan to wash their faces in the cool creek water from the bucket.

"You won't have to say 'eat' twice to me this morning. I'm starving!" Joe joked as he sat down across from Uncle Ned.

The girls joined them, and the Indian woman placed bowls of steaming hot oats and slices of homemade bread, with thick slices of ham between, in front of them. Elizabeth filled the coffee cups and passed them around.

"Good morning, Morning Star," Mandie smiled as she caught the old squaw's hand. The Indian woman smiled too and patted the girl's long blonde curls.

"Love," she whispered, and Mandie returned the word.

"Love. Oh, Morning Star, you are learning English!"

Sallie was listening. "She can understand some of what you say in English, but I have never heard her say an English word before. You are a good influence, Mandie."

After the chores were done and the noon meal eaten, the three wandered outside, waiting for Tsa'ni. Soon he arrived, carrying a lantern.

"Sallie, get the lantern from your grandfather's barn, too. It will be dark in the cave," Tsa'ni told her.

Sallie got the lantern and gave it to Joe to carry.

"Ready?" Tsa'ni asked.

"Yes, but I should tell my mother that we are going now," Mandie told him.

"Never mind. I will tell your mother, and your grand-father, Sallie." The Indian boy hurried up to the open door of the cabin with Mandie right behind him. Looking inside, he said, "I am taking the boy and the girl to see the mountain, the woods, and the creek. Sallie is going with us."

Elizabeth spoke up. "How kind of you, Tsa'ni. Amanda, you won't be long, will you?"

"No, Mother," she replied, turning to join the others waiting in the yard. "Tsa'ni, you didn't mention the cave."

"That is all right. The cave is included in the mountain and the woods. Come, let us go." He started off down the road toward the creek.

Mandie picked up Snowball and carried him on her shoulder. At first it was great fun, skipping along by the creek bank, throwing pebbles at the fish, plucking wild flowers, chasing butterflies, but after a while it became an uphill climb, and it was beginning to get hot. There was no definite trail, but Tsa'ni seemed to know the way all right. The other three grew more quiet and slowed their pace as they became more and more exhausted.

"Whew! Tsa'ni, how much farther?" Mandie complained, holding her skirt close to her legs through the thick undergrowth.

The Indian boy laughed. "Not far."

"Not far to you must mean miles to us," Joe sighed, as he pushed a brier away from his pant leg.

"Tsa'ni, where *are* you taking us?" Sallie demanded.

"To the cave, Sallie. I know the way," the boy replied.

Mandie turned to the Indian girl. "Don't *you* know

where the cave is, Sallie?"

"No, I have only heard of it. I do not wander around the way the boys do." Sallie smiled. "And I have not lived long with my grandfather, so I do not know this land."

"Do not worry. I will not get you lost. I know exactly where we are going," Tsa'ni assured them.

A long time later a rushing, roaring waterfall came into view. Mandie stopped to admire it.

"Oh, how beautiful!" she exclaimed.

"That is where we are going," Tsa'ni told her.

He ran ahead of them and when they reached the falls, he stopped and gave them directions. "Now, you must walk across the rocks in the creek behind the waterfall. The entrance to the cave is behind the falls," and he started forward.

"We'll get all wet!" Mandie screamed above the noise of the water.

"No, you will not get wet if you stay against the cliff away from the water when you walk through. Just watch where you step. The rocks are slippery sometimes," Tsa'ni yelled back and continued on.

Mandie followed, with Sallie behind her, and Joe bringing up the rear. Snowball was frightened of the water and clung desperately to Mandie's shoulder.

Once under the falls, Mandie looked up and could see a ledge protecting the walkway as the water cascaded down into the creek. It felt terribly damp under there and the rocks were awfully slippery. There was no use trying to talk. No one could be heard above the sound of the water.

Joe lost his footing once, and if the girls hadn't grabbed for him, he would have fallen into the creek. The slip caused the girls to almost lose their balance, and

Mandie felt her free hand scrape a rock as she grabbed for a hold. Regaining her footing, she stuck her hand out into the waterfall to wash away the grit and slime. The water was ice cold.

Tsa'ni had stopped ahead of them, and when they caught up they found him waiting in front of a huge, dark hole in the cliff which appeared to be the mouth of the cave. He had taken a match from his pocket and was lighting his lantern, motioning for Joe to light the one he carried, and then he entered the cave.

Once inside, the loud roar of the falls became a muffled sound and Mandie looked around, afraid to go any farther. Joe, right behind her and Sallie, swung the lantern around, lighting up the cave. They could see huge, moss-covered boulders around the entrance. The floor seemed to be solid rock.

"Come!" Tsa'ni called, going deeper into the cave. "I want to show you something."

The three hurried on, passing into another part of the cave with enormous, long spears of rock hanging from the ceiling and sprouting up from the floor. They looked around in wonder.

"What are those things?" Mandie asked, breathlessly.

"That is what I wanted to show you. The ones hanging from overhead are stalactites and the ones sitting on the ground are called stalagmites," Tsa'ni explained.

"Well, what caused them?" Joe asked.

"They are formed by the water dripping from above," the Indian boy replied.

"It must have taken an awfully long time," Sallie remarked.

"Hundreds of years, maybe thousands," Tsa'ni nodded.

Mandie set Snowball down, and he began to check out the scent of the floor.

"You mean this cave has been here that long?" Mandie asked.

"And this is the cave where Tsali lived?" Sallie queried.

"Yes. People are born, live, and die, but mountains stay forever," the Indian boy replied. "This cave has several tunnels and other sections. Come, I will show you."

The group followed as he went down a long tunnel which led into another section of the cave, and then continued into another tunnel. It was all so dark and cold. The lanterns made a soft glow and cast eerie shadows. Snowball seemed nervous. He leaned against Mandie's skirt and meowed to be picked up. She consented and he snuggled against her shoulder.

"Oh, Snowball, I think you are lazy today," she laughed.

"Look, there is a stream over there. Look closely and you can see minnows in it," Tsa'ni told them, pointing to the other side of the large cavern they were in.

Everyone hurried over to the stream and huddled on the ground to watch for minnows in the flowing water.

Tsa'ni, with a sly grin on his face, silently crept away, heading for the entrance. He knew his way around inside, and the trail for home, but he knew the two white children didn't know the way, and neither did Sallie. *The white girl claims to be part Indian*, he thought. *Well, we'll just see how much Indian she is. A real Indian could find the way out. White people—always coming to mess in Cherokee business!*

Joe turned to speak to Tsa'ni. "I don't see any minnows." And then realizing the Indian boy was nowhere in sight, he called, "*Tsa'ni*, where are you?"

The girls were startled at the alarm in Joe's voice. They saw no sign of Tsa'ni. Mandie once again felt the hatred rising in her heart.

"He has left us!" Sallie spoke angrily.

"Oh, no, Sallie! How will we ever find the way out— and home?" Mandie cried.

"We can only search around and hope to see familiar things," the Indian girl told them.

"Thank goodness, we have a lantern," Joe added.

Mandie sighed. "Well, let's be on our way." She started forward and then stopped. "Joe, you'd better go first with the lantern so we can watch our step."

"Please, be careful," Joe warned them. He stepped ahead and flashed the light into the next section of the cave. "Did we come in from here or over there? There's another opening over there." His voice echoed.

The girls turned to look. There *was* another opening. They were both puzzled.

"This one, I—I think," Mandie said, indicating the one nearest where they stood.

"No, I think it is that one over there," Sallie disagreed.

"Hey, now, we can't go two ways at once," Joe said.

"All right, which way do you say, Joe? We'll go the way two of us agree on," Mandie said.

"I just don't know!" Joe sounded confused. "I suppose we could *try* this way and then come back if we don't find the way out."

"And maybe get thoroughly lost doing it!" Mandie moaned.

"But there is nothing else we can do but try," Sallie reasoned.

"Agreed," Joe said. "So here we go." He led the way

into the next cavern, and to their dismay it had several openings.

"Listen for the sound of the water," Sallie told them. "If we can get headed toward the water, we will find our way out."

The three stood still, holding their breath, listening for the faint roar of the waterfall. Simultaneously they pointed in three different directions. Then they all laughed.

"I've always heard two heads are better than one, but I'm not so sure three heads are any good at all," Mandie sighed.

"Let's do it this way," Joe suggested. "We'll take turns deciding which way to go."

"All right, you choose first," Sallie replied.

"This way," Joe said, pointing to his right, and the girls followed.

Now they were in a long tunnel with no end in sight within the dim light of the lantern.

"Mandie, you choose next," Sallie said, as they stumbled along the rough floor.

"Right now I would choose to go back the other way. It looked smoother and I don't remember a floor as rough as this one. No, wait! I see a dark place on the right up there." She hurried forward. "It's an opening!"

"Well, let's go through it," Joe said, flashing the lantern light inside the next cavern. At that moment it seemed like hundreds of dark birds came flying at them. Flapping wings buzzed around their heads and a wild cackling sound filled the air. Joe and Mandie froze in terror.

"Bats!" Sallie yelled. "Get down low and go back out!"

The three almost crawled out of the cavern into the tunnel they had just come down. Two of the bats circled here and there, and then disappeared.

"Sorry, I picked the wrong way," Mandie said breathlessly, as they ran through the tunnel.

"Here is another opening on the left," Sallie said. "Joe, hold the light inside first so we can see."

Joe flashed the lantern around but no bats appeared. Directly across the passageway was yet another opening. "There's another tunnel over there."

The girls followed him on through. It was a large cavern with a huge hole in the middle of the floor. They gathered around to look. Even though Joe held the lantern as far over the hole as he could bend, they could not see the bottom.

"Oh, how spooky!" Mandie shrieked.

"Do not get too near the edge!" Sallie warned them.

Joe turned to look at the girls. "I think we are completely lost."

"That Tsa'ni! Just wait until I tell my grandfather what he has done to us!" Sallie cried.

"There's only one thing left to do," Mandie told them. "We must pray. In fact, we should have prayed long before now."

"Pray?" asked Sallie.

"Yes. I know you must go to church, because Uncle Ned does. Whenever I am afraid or confused I ask God to help me," Mandie told her. "And He always does."

"Yes, I go to church and I believe in God," the Indian girl replied.

"Then, let's all repeat this verse together: 'What time I am afraid I will put my trust in Thee.'" And the three did as Mandie suggested.

"Oh, dear God, please help us! We need your help now!" Mandie pleaded, turning her eyes upward.

"Now let's not worry anymore. God will help us find the way out," Joe added.

"Yes, but I cannot hear Him telling us which way to go, can you?" Sallie was serious as she looked at the other two.

"No, but we have to trust Him to put it into our heads which way to go," Mandie explained.

"I think I'll check what's over on the other side," Joe said, walking slowly around the huge hole in the floor.

The wall on the other side had stones of all shapes and sizes piled up against it, and there was no opening.

Mandie, following Joe, accidentally stubbed her toe on a rock near the bottom of the pile, and all of a sudden the whole stack seemed about to tumble. She jumped out of the way and bent to look closer at the stones. As she was straightening up, her eyes caught a glitter in the pile.

"Joe, hold the lantern over here! I saw something shiny in the rocks!" she exclaimed.

"Oh, it's probably mica," Joe said.

As he swung the lantern the light revealed more glitter and the three began pulling at the rocks to see what was there, breaking fingernails and rolling rocks onto their shoes. All at once a large stone rolled down, uncovering a pile of gold nuggets.

"Gold!" whistled Joe, furiously digging away the loose stones.

"Gold!" murmured Mandie.

"Gold!" repeated Sallie.

Then the three of them broke into hysterical laughter.

"Here we are, lost to civilization, with a fortune in gold at our feet!" Mandie cried, picking up a nugget.

"Yes, we'd better be trying to find our way out," Sallie reminded them.

"Find our way out? Oh, Sallie, aren't you interested in seeing how much gold is here behind the rocks?" Joe asked, as he kept digging.

"Gold—that is what caused the Cherokees to lose their land, their homes—everything!" Sallie replied, sadly.

Mandie turned to her, understanding. "I know, Sallie. If that gold had not been found in Georgia, the white people might not have ever made the Cherokees move out." She dropped the nugget into her pocket.

"Daylight! I see daylight!" shouted Joe as he continued to pull away at the rocks. "There's an outside opening behind all these rocks!" In his excitement he broke the lantern on a rock he was rolling away and they were suddenly in the dark.

But he was right. Together the three soon had a hole dug big enough for them to squeeze through to the outside. The terror of being lost in the dark, cold cave was over.

"It's a little uphill out there, I think. Let me go first and then I can help you two crawl out," Joe suggested.

All thought of the gold left their minds. Joe climbed through the hole they had dug and pulled the two girls after him. Snowball scrambled ahead of Mandie. Sallie went through last and barely cleared her foot when the whole side of the cave seemed to come tumbling down and the opening disappeared.

"Thank you, God! Thank you!" Mandie cried.

"Amen!" Joe added.

"Me, too!" Sallie said.

They stood up and looked around. They were in a thick forest of balsam firs and it seemed to be growing dark rapidly. Hours must have passed since they left Uncle Ned's house and now they were lost in the woods. There was no sign of the waterfall or the creek. It would be dark soon, and they had no lantern.

Chapter 3 / Captured in the Dark

Tsa'ni waited for hours outside under the waterfall for the three to find their way out of the cave, but they never came out. He smiled to himself. *That white girl claimed to be part Cherokee. If she was part Cherokee she would find the way out.* He sat down to whittle on a piece of pine he took from his pocket. It got later and later and then began to grow dark, and still there was no sign of the three!

Suddenly he heard voices and saw lights flashing through the waterfall in front of him as they came nearer. He stood up and put his knife and the piece of wood back into his pocket. Evidently a search party was coming and he had better be prepared for them.

A group of men appeared through the trees, swinging lanterns in the dark. One stepped forward and Tsa'ni recognized him as Uncle Ned.

"Cave under water," he said, motioning to the waterfall. "Papooses might go there."

Uncle John walked to the edge of the creek, swinging a lantern. "Where is the cave, Uncle Ned? I can't see a thing beyond the water."

"Follow me," the old Indian told the others. He took them across the rocks and under the waterfall.

Then they were face to face with Tsa'ni.

"Tsa'ni! Where Papooses?" Uncle Ned demanded.

"We went into the cave and they ran off and left me. I went back inside to look for them, but could not find them," the Indian boy lied to the old man.

"Lost in cave!" Uncle Ned muttered.

"Do you know your way around in there?" asked Uncle John as the old Indian approached the entrance and flashed his lantern light inside.

"Little," Uncle Ned replied. "Big place, many rooms. Drumgool, pull trees. We make trail." He spoke in Cherokee to another Indian in the group.

Drumgool, understanding his friend's language, turned back and ordered the other men to gather small branches from the trees. Soon they returned with their arms full, while Uncle Ned and Uncle John waited at the entrance to the cave.

"We make trail," the old Indian repeated, entering the tunnel into the cave. The other Indians, understanding perfectly what he meant, began breaking twigs from the branches they carried and dropping them on the floor as they followed him.

Tsa'ni followed along in the rear. Now that the three were really lost, he was afraid of what they might tell. He had better prepare a good argument for when they were found. *Palefaces, why didn't they stay out of Cherokee territory? Always causing trouble!* He thought to himself.

Led by Uncle Ned, with Uncle John close behind, the search party thoroughly combed the cave.

"No one come to cave anymore. Rocks slide," Uncle

Ned said, pointing to a rockpile that had evidently fallen from above in one of the sections.

"But Tsa'ni, knowing this, took them inside?" Uncle John questioned.

"Tsa'ni bad brave!" Uncle Ned was angry.

"I don't think the boy likes us, even though we are kinpeople," replied Uncle John as they entered another tunnel.

"Tsa'ni no like white people," Uncle Ned explained. "He have no heart." He swung his lantern up and another rockpile came into sight. "Rocks dangerous."

"Where, oh, where can those kids be?" John sighed. "Tsa'ni said they ran off and left him while they were in the cave. Maybe they are already outside somewhere, or have already gone back to the house."

"Papooses come home; Morning Star send word. No, Papooses not home," the old man said as he flashed his light into the room with the huge hole in the floor. The opening the young ones had dug in the wall to escape through was now completely obliterated, and a pile of rocks hid the gold nuggets. "Papooses not here."

They went into the other sections and surprised the bats as the three lost ones had done.

Tsa'ni, still tagging along at the rear, was growing more and more positive that the three had just completely disappeared. He knew only the one way in and out of the cave, and they had certainly not come out. On the other hand, they weren't to be found in the cave. They had just vanished.

It was a big cave and the men were tired, but Uncle Ned insisted on going through the entire place one more time. This time the men laid bare twigs for their trail. They walked slowly and poked into every crevice, looked into every nook and cranny, and finally ended up back at their starting place.

Uncle Ned shook his head in dismay. "Not here. Now we look in trees, bushes," he told the men, explaining how they would work.

"Please, God, let us find them before some harm comes to them," Uncle John implored, as they gathered to leave the cave.

Mandie, Sallie, and Joe stumbled along in the dark-ness after they left the cave. It was some time before their eyes became accustomed to the dark night so that they could detect outlines of bushes and trees.

"Where do you think we are, Sallie? Do you have any idea?" Joe asked.

"I do not know this land, but I think we should keep going downhill because we went uphill all the way to the cave," she replied, pushing the limbs of a bush out of her face.

Mandie, carrying Snowball on her shoulder, was hav-ing the roughest time of all because the kitten insisted on clinging to her dress; and every time she took an uneven step because of unlevel ground or rocks and underbrush in the way, Snowball tightened his claws. And with the nightfall, it had become cold on the North Carolina mountain.

"I hope we're not too far away from food. I'm hungry!" Joe exclaimed.

"Me, too," Mandie added. "And I'm cold."

"Here is food," Sallie said, stopping by a huge bush and pulling berries from its limbs. "Serviceberries. They are good to eat."

"Oh, yes," agreed Mandie as she and Joe joined the Indian girl for a berry supper. They sat down on a boulder nearby. She offered one to Snowball. He turned his nose away from it. "Snowball, if you don't want these berries, you're going to have to wait, and no telling how long."

"Cats don't eat berries, Mandie," Joe laughed at her.

"Well, Snowball eats tomatoes, so why can't he eat berries?" Mandie told him. "Goodness gracious, I'm tired." She took a deep breath and stretched.

"Me, too, but we must keep moving on. There may be dangerous animals here," Sallie told them as she stood up.

"Of course! And we don't have a thing to defend ourselves," Joe said, as he and Mandie got to their feet and Snowball clung to the shoulder of Mandie's dress.

"Joe, what did we do in that cave?" Mandie admonished him. "We said we would trust in God. Have you forgotten so soon?"

"Well, no, but it would help if we had a rifle," he answered.

"Since we do not have one, I suggest we make haste," Sallie said, going ahead downhill through the bushes. The other two quickly followed.

It was a cloudy night with no moon to light the way. The three hurried along, slipping, sliding, sometimes falling over huge boulders along the path they took, sometimes getting caught in the briers of a bush, sometimes being struck in the face by an unseen branch. On Sallie's advice they tried to keep on a downhill route, but it was so dark and the trees and brush were so thick, they could not be sure which way they were going.

A small animal brushed by Sallie's legs in the darkness, and in her fright she lost her balance and went sliding downhill straight into a stream. Mandie and Joe ran after her.

"Here I am. Here!" the Indian girl called to them as

she rose from the edge of the water. Luckily the wet sand had stopped her and only her feet had gone into the water.

"I can't see you," Joe called.

"Keep talking," Mandie told her. "We'll follow your voice." She put Snowball down so she could hurry.

"I landed in a stream down here," Sallie called to them.

"I can hear you," Joe yelled back to her. He went running down the hill and suddenly ran into what sounded like a bunch of huge tin cans.

Mandie, frightened by the noise, called out. "Joe, are you all right? What was that noise?"

"Looks like a whole lot of big cans," he said, as Mandie and Sallie both got to his side.

The Indian girl walked slowly around, feeling the cans and trying to see in the darkness. "I think it is a still."

"A still?" asked Mandie.

"A real moonshine still?" asked Joe.

"That means someone has been here and may be somewhere close around," Mandie figured.

"Sure does, and it means they must be bootleggers," Joe laughed.

Sallie did not understand his language. "Bootleggers?"

"Yeh, that's people who make liquor illegally," the boy said.

"Bad Cherokees make liquor, but not here," Sallie replied.

They were talking loudly enough that their voices carried in the dark, still night.

Mandie cautioned them. "The bootleggers might be around. We'd better be quiet. You've already made enough noise banging against those tin cans."

Out of the darkness a pair of hands grabbed Joe from behind and at the same time another pair latched onto Sallie, pushing her against Mandie and causing the girls to fall. The two dark forms were barely visible.

"Hey, what are you doing to me?" Joe demanded, as he felt his hands being tied behind him. He put up a struggle but the hands were too strong.

"They ain't nothin' but younguns, Snuff," a woman's coarse voice said as she held onto the two girls.

There was a strong, sickening smell about the two strangers. Evidently they had been drinking what they made in the still.

"Ne'er mind what they be, they done found somethin' that ain't none of their bidness and they's aliable to be atellin' the wrong people 'bout it," Snuff replied as he finished tying Joe's hands, and with the end of the long rope started to tie Sallie's as well, leaving a short piece of rope between the two.

"Please, Mr. Snuff, we won't tell anyone we saw you, or whatever it is you don't want us to tell," begged Mandie, the woman still holding her tightly.

"No, we'll just do as you say, Mr. Snuff," put in Joe.

"Shet up!" Snuff replied.

"Y'see, Snuff, they don't even know what we're atalkin' about," the woman told him.

"Shet your smacker, too, Rennie Lou," the man said. He jerked Mandie's hand from the woman, causing the girl to slip as he jerked her around. She almost fell head first into a bush. As she stumbled, her hair ribbon fell out and caught on a twig unnoticed.

Snuff pulled Mandie's hand behind her, and leaving a short space in the rope for Sallie's hands, he tied Mandie's, letting the long end of the rope dangle. Now all three were tied to the same rope.

"We are lost," Sallie tried to explain. "We do not even know where we are. If you would just show us the way back to Deep Creek, we would be most grateful."

Snuff turned quickly to look at Sallie in the darkness. "An Injun, by George! We've captured an Injun here!"

"Now, how do you know? It's so dark I can't even tell what color hair they've got," Rennie Lou said.

"Don't you catch that Injun accent? No matter how much eddication they git, you kin always hear that kind of lisp they have," Snuff said, trying to look closely at Sallie in the dark.

"Yes, you are right. I am Cherokee," Sallie proudly told him, as she tried to straighten up in pride.

"Well, well, well, whadda ya know!" Rennie Lou slapped her skirt and laughed hoarsely. "And is the udder two Injuns, too?"

Snuff was trying to see what the other two looked like but it was too dark.

"Nope, don't think so. That 'un has got yellar hair," he said. "Well, now that you'ins can't git away too well, mind tellin' me whar you thought you was goin' this time o' night?"

"Sallie told you the truth, Mr. Snuff. We are lost," Joe replied.

"That's right. We are," Mandie added.

"Lost? Everybody that believes that stand on your head," the man growled. He pulled the rope, almost causing the three to lose their balance. "Now, where was you'ins goin'?"

"We were in the cave and got lost," Sallie told him. "There are probably search parties out right now looking for us."

"In the cave? What cave?" the man asked.

"The cave where the Indian Charley hid," Mandie told him.

"The cave whar the whut?" he howled and stomped his foot. "Now that's a good 'un. Ain't no cave nowhere 'round hyar, much less an Injun called Charley."

"Well, we were in a cave," Joe said, "whether you believe it or not. We were in a cave."

"I know every leaf and stone in these hyar woods. Ain't no cave hyar," the old man argued.

"But Joe's right. We were in a cave. The Indian boy with us ran off and left us and we got lost," Mandie insisted.

"Snuff," the woman said as the old man jerked Mandie around on the rope. "Make 'em show us if thar's a cave. A cave might come in handy sometime."

"All right. We'll keep 'em in the barn till daylight and then they will show us the cave," Snuff agreed, pushing the three together in front of him. "This way. Rennie Lou, lead the way and watch out for any sudden-like tricks."

O God, please help us! Mandie prayed silently as they were herded forward. She had never been so scared in all her life. The old man and woman didn't seem to have any common sense about anything, and there was no telling what they might do to them. Besides, everyone would be out looking for them, and her mother would be awfully worried.

They stumbled about in the darkness trying to follow the woman as they were ordered to do. Snowball, unseen by the man and woman, scampered along near Mandie. All three were already tired, hungry, and worn out. Now they were about to collapse from their weariness in avoiding the branches that scratched their faces and the thorns and briers that tore their clothes. Mandie slipped on a rock and pulled the other two down with her as she fell.

"Now, look ahyar. None of that stuff!" the old man yelled, jerking cruelly at the rope. "You're agoin' to the barn whether you like it or not. Git up! Now! Rennie Lou, give 'em a hand!"

The old woman tried to help in the dark but she wasn't much help. They finally managed to get to their feet.

"I'm sorry, Sallie, Joe. I accidentally fell. I didn't do it on purpose," Mandie apologized.

"It's all right, Mandie," Joe calmed her.

"It could have happened to either one of us," Sallie said, as they moved on.

Soon they could make out the blurred outline of a building in the clearing ahead. As they came closer they could see it was a rough log cabin, and to their dismay they were pushed on past it. Snowball followed.

"Go on! This ain't the barn," Snuff told them.

"Ain't far," Rennie Lou looked back and informed them.

After passing a clump of bushes behind the house, another structure showed up in the darkness. Rennie Lou walked on toward it and stopped at the door. She swung it open on creaky hinges.

"All right, inside!" Snuff prodded them on through the doorway into the darkness.

"Want me to light the lantern, Snuff?" the woman asked.

"Course not, woman. You want them to see us?" the old man growled. He pushed the three forward. "There's a pile of hay over thar. You kin sleep thar till it gits daylight!"

"Could we have a drink of water?" Joe asked. "We haven't had any food or water since noon yesterday."

"Water? Well, reckon you kin. Rennie Lou, git the water bucket over thar," Snuff said.

The woman picked up something in the darkness and came toward them. Joe felt a metal bucket in her hands as she pushed it in his face. "Hyar you air. Sorry we ain't got no dipper," she said. "But I tell you whut. There's apples in that haystack if you kin manage to eat one without usin' yer hands!" She laughed hysterically, holding the bucket to Joe's mouth.

"Rennie Lou, leave 'em be," Snuff warned her. Turning back to the three captives, he said, "Now we'll be back as soon as the sun cracks that darkness. Meantime you'd better rest good 'cause you're gonna find that cave for us, or else."

The man and the woman left the barn then, slamming the door behind them. The three prisoners gave a sigh of relief. Snowball moved around Mandie's feet.

"Now, we've got to think fast," Joe whispered to the others. "How can we get loose? We've got to get loose before they come back, so we can get away."

"Yes, they are definitely drunk," Mandie agreed. "I'm afraid of people who drink liquor."

"You never know what they will do when they have been drinking spirits," Sallie said. "But what can we do?"

"Oh, I don't know offhand but I suggest we start thinking," Joe replied. "I have no idea how you go about sitting down when you are all tied together like we are, but why don't we just take a plop all together?"

"All right, on count of three we'll all sit at once," Mandie agreed.

"One, two, three!" Together they landed in a pile of hay in the dark. Snowball prowled around them and started playing with the end of the rope hanging from Mandie's hands.

"We'll never be able to get up again," Sallie told them.

"We've got an awful lot of thinking to do first," Joe said.

"Yes, we've got to get back to Uncle Ned's, so we can go back to the cave and get the gold," Mandie reminded them.

"I do not want any of that gold, but I will go with you," Sallie told her.

"Yeh, we've got to get back to that gold somehow. There must be a fortune there," Joe said.

"I wonder who put it there," Mandie mused as she twisted her hands in the rope. "Do you suppose these people here did?" Snowball's paw caught at the rope behind her.

"No, because they don't even know about the cave," Joe said.

"Maybe some bank robbers left it there," Mandie suggested.

"I doubt it because it is too hard to get to the cave from any road or trail," the Indian girl replied. "Besides, they would probably guard it. And Tsa'ni seems to know his way around in there."

"You don't mean *he* could have put it there?" asked Mandie.

"No, he would never have gold like that," Sallie answered. "I mean someone would have seen him around if they were guarding the gold."

"You're right. But how did it get there? And who put it there?" Joe asked.

"We could ask Uncle Ned about it," Mandie said.

"First, we have to get away from these people, so we'd better concentrate on that," Joe reminded the two girls.

It was going to take an awful lot of thinking to get them out of their predicament.

Chapter 4 / Dimar

Elizabeth Shaw could sit still no longer waiting for her daughter to come back or to be found. It was a long time after midnight and no word had come from anyone. She decided it was time she helped in the search.

"Morning Star," she began, trying to talk to the old squaw. "You and me—" she pointed to the squaw and to herself—"let's go to Bird-town and get Mandie's kinpeople to help find them."

Morning Star understood part of it. "Bird-town," she said.

Elizabeth smiled and made motions like she was riding a horse and then pointed to the old woman and to herself again. "Bird-town," she said again.

The Indian woman grinned as she understood what Elizabeth meant. She got up and motioned to Elizabeth to follow her. She went outside to the barn. There was a small cart inside and Morning Star hastily opened a door to a stall and led out a pony. Elizabeth helped her harness it to the cart and they started out for Bird-town.

Meanwhile the three prisoners in the barn were still talking and trying to figure out a way to escape from the old man and woman.

"If we could only see in this darkness, we might find something we could cut the rope with," Mandie said.

"How is either one of us going to cut the rope when all our hands are tied?" Joe wanted to know.

"If one of us had something we could hold in our hands, we could back up to each other and cut each other's ropes apart," Sallie said.

"That's right," Mandie replied and then jumped as Snowball clawed her hand as he played with the rope. "Oh, Snowball, you stuck me with your claws!" Then she caught her breath. "Snowball! Snowball! He can do it!"

"Do what, Mandie?" Joe asked.

"Untie the rope. If I shake it for him to play with, he can claw at it until it comes undone!"

"Oh, Mandie, how could a cat untie a rope?" Joe asked.

"Well, it does feel looser and besides, I am the last one on the rope." She shook her hands behind her, and Snowball jumped and began playing and clawing at the rope.

"Mandie, it'll never work," Joe told her.

"Snowball is smarter than you give him credit for. Don't forget, I am the one who educated him," laughed Mandie, still shaking her hands as the kitten played. "It's looser! It's looser!"

"Please keep trying," Sallie told her as she shifted from her cramped position to lean back against a post. Then she jumped forward again. A nail had scratched her back. "Mandie, there's a nail behind me. If Snowball has the rope loose enough, you might be able to hang it on the nail and pull it apart."

"Where, Sallie, where?" Mandie was excited.

"Do not lose your sense of direction. It is directly behind me on the post. I am going to move so you can slide over here in my place," the Indian girl said, moving slowly closer to Joe, who began edging farther away to give the girls room to move. Mandie kept sliding until she felt the post behind her. She leaned back trying to locate the nail.

"I've found it!" she cried. "Now if I can just catch the rope on it!" She maneuvered her hands until her fingers found the nail, and then she slid her wrists around until the nail caught the rope.

"Did you find it?" Joe wanted to know. "Or I should say, did the nail find the rope?"

"Yes, now I have the rope caught on it. If I can only catch the right loop so it will start untying."

"Be careful. You might hurt yourself," Sallie warned her.

Snowball had followed Mandie and was again pulling at the rope with his claws. One foot caught and he pulled with all his might trying to get his paw free. Mandie felt the rope give way. She rubbed her wrists together and slipped one hand out of the noose.

"It worked! I have my left hand free!" she cried. "There! I have it all off! Now, let me get you two untied."

She slipped behind Sallie and freed her hands and then removed the rope from Joe's hands. The three sat there rubbing their bruised wrists in the dark.

"That man must not have tied the knots very tight," Joe said.

"Probably because he was too drunk to realize what he was doing," the Indian girl said.

"Well, let's get going!" Mandie stood up, picking up Snowball.

"I will leave a signal for our people if they come here

looking for us," Sallie said, as she removed the beads from around her neck and hung them on the nail. "My grandfather will see these and will know we were here."

"I hope we find them before they get this far," Joe said.

"We'd certainly better be careful going by the log cabin," Mandie reminded them as they stepped out of the barn. The first signs of dawn were in the sky.

"We will circle the clearing and stay away from the house," the Indian girl told them. She led the way, keeping the house at a distance as they tried to find their way back into the woods and downhill.

While the three were trying to find their way, Uncle Ned's search party had fanned out across the mountain. He and Uncle John stayed together while the other men scattered out. Sometime later the old Indian found the bright blue ribbon from Mandie's hair hanging on the bush by the creek where she had lost it in the scuffle with the old man and woman.

"Papoose ribbon!" he cried excitedly as he pulled the ribbon from the bush. "They been here!" He looked around on the ground. "Feet make marks!" He pointed to the footprints in the soft sand by the water.

Uncle John anxiously bent to look.

"Looks like quite a few different feet," he remarked.

"Yes," the old Indian said, as he straightened up to follow the direction of the footprints. "Go this way." He walked on up the hill, bending low to see the prints as he continued. The old cabin came into view.

"At least we know they got out of the cave," Uncle John said.

"I hear people coming," Uncle Ned said, listening as he turned his ear toward the sound. "Walk like white people."

Snuff and Rennie Lou appeared in the distance, their heavy shoes noisily clopping on the rocks here and there. Uncle Ned stepped behind a tree and motioned for Uncle John to do the same.

As the couple drew nearer, the old Indian stepped out directly in front of them. They stopped in their tracks.

"Where Papoose—wear this ribbon?" Uncle Ned held up Mandie's ribbon for them to see.

"What papoose?" Snuff asked. "We ain't seen no papoose, Injun."

"Papoose feet make prints to your house," Uncle Ned said, pointing to the tracks in the dirt. "Where Papoose?"

Rennie Lou held tightly onto Snuff's arm. She was frightened of the old Indian. Snuff tried to bluff his way out.

"I told you we ain't seen no papoose. Now git out of our way!" Snuff gave Uncle Ned a shove.

At that instant Uncle John, his rifle in his hand, stepped out from behind another tree and Uncle Ned gave a loud whistle to round up his braves. The man and woman stood still without saying a word. Indians came from every direction out of the woods as they heard their leader's call for help. Snuff and Rennie Lou, quaking in their boots, were soon surrounded.

"Hold man, woman," Uncle Ned ordered. "Me and John—we go look." The circle of Indians closed in around the frightened pair.

Following the footprints, Uncle Ned and John went on past the cabin and into the barn. The old Indian looked around and grunted as he picked up Sallie's beads from the nail on the post.

"Papooses been here," he said to Uncle John, holding up the beads.

"But evidently they are gone now," Uncle John replied.

"Left different way. Prints going opposite way," Uncle Ned said, motioning to the footprints left by the three as they had detoured around the house.

Suddenly the dark, cloudy sky broke loose and the rain came pouring down. The old Indian looked up in dismay.

"Rain wash feet marks away!" he exclaimed. "Must hurry!"

"And the children are out in this," Uncle John fretted. "Unless they found the way back, which I doubt very much."

The old man whistled for his braves once more and they came on the run, pushing the man and woman along with them in the downpour.

"Must hurry. Rain clean trail," Uncle Ned told them. "We follow feet marks now!" He pointed to the footprints remaining in the sand.

"What we do with palefaces?" Drumgool asked, pushing the two forward.

"Let go. Must hurry," the old Indian instructed him.

"I think we should send the authorities back up here, Uncle Ned," John said. "These people are kidnappers!"

Uncle Ned nodded in agreement.

Snuff and Rennie Lou heard all that was said and looked at each other anxiously. They were sober this morning and the realization of their crime began to dawn on them.

"Look, we ain't meant no harm. We didn't hurt the younguns," Snuff pleaded. "In fact, we'll hep you hunt 'em if you want."

"No! We don't need your help," Uncle John told them, firmly. "You have broken the law. It will all be taken care of as I said. I am reporting this to the authorities. You're not going to get away with it."

"Please, mister," the woman begged. "We won't never do it again. I 'spect we jest had too much partyin' 'fore they showed up. We didn't hardly know whut we was doin'. Can't you unnerstan' that?"

John shook his head and ran to follow Uncle Ned, with the braves bringing up the rear. The rain was quickly obliterating the tracks of the three, and they were hurrying as fast as they could go. Their clothing was heavy with the dampness, and the wet rocks had become slippery, but they knew they were on the trail of the missing children.

Far ahead of them, Mandie, Joe, and Sallie pushed their way through the dripping bushes and mostly slid downhill when they came to huge boulders now and then. Snowball registered his complaint by clinging tightly to Mandie's dress.

"Sallie, do you think we are heading in the right direction?" Mandie asked.

"I am not certain but I do know we are headed toward the foot of the mountain, and once we get down there we'll be able to find the way home," the girl replied.

"Whew! I'm still hungry!" Joe complained as he led the way. "We sure were dumb not to load up with apples from that barn."

"It's too late now," Mandie replied. "When we get back to Uncle Ned's I'm going to eat everything in the house." She laughed, tossing her long, wet hair back out of her face.

"Even owl stew?" Joe teased her.

"I said everything," she replied.

"Everyone must be worried about us by now," Sallie said. "I am certain my grandfather has a party searching—if we only knew which direction they were coming from."

"Looks like a level place for a while here," Joe remarked as they came down into a meadow.

At that moment an arrow suddenly shot through the trees near Mandie, who was carrying the kitten. Snowball, frightened by the sudden movement, jumped down and darted ahead. He ran up the first tree he came to and peered down from a limb.

Mandie, not noticing the kitten, stared and pointed to the arrow imbedded in another tree. "Joe! Sallie! Look!"

"Land o'Goshen, don't stand there! Come on!" Joe grabbed her hand and turned to grip Sallie's hand. They ran along until they came to a thick clump of bushes, where they hid. From there they saw a young Indian appear in the clearing and go to the arrow in the tree.

Sallie immediately felt relief. She was certain the boy would help them. She broke out of the bushes, calling back, "That is an Indian boy. He will help us. Come on!" She ran toward the boy. "We are lost! Please help us!"

Mandie and Joe, not trusting the boy, stayed behind the bushes. The boy turned to look at Sallie. "Where did you come from?"

"I am Sallie Sweetwater. My friends and I are lost. Will you help us?" she asked as she stood before the boy who seemed to be not much older than she was.

The boy looked around. "Your friends? Where are they?"

"They are behind the bushes because you almost hit us with your arrow and they are frightened," she told him.

"I am very sorry. I will not harm any of you. Tell them to come out," he said.

Sallie called to her friends. "Come on, Mandie, Joe.

He will help us find the way!"

Mandie and Joe reluctantly appeared from their shelter and came forward. The boy's eyes lit up when he saw the blonde-haired girl.

She is the most beautiful girl I have ever seen, he was thinking as she came nearer. *And blue eyes! How beautiful!*

Mandie returned his stare, thinking what a handsome boy he was!

"Where are you going?" the boy asked.

"We are trying to find the way to Deep Creek where I live with my grandfather," Sallie told him.

"Deep Creek!" he repeated. "You are going in the wrong direction!"

"Oh, no!" Joe moaned. "I'm starving to death!"

"Yes," the boy said. "My name is Dimar Walkingstick. I live with my mother not far from here. I will take you to her for food and dry clothes. Come!" He turned, expecting them to follow him.

"I am certain my grandfather has a search party looking for us by now," the Indian girl said. "We shall leave a trail for him."

"Of course. I will go ahead and break the twigs as we go. He will see them and find the way to my house," Dimar said, as he began marking their way.

"Food!" Joe murmured. "At last, some food!"

"That's what he said," Mandie replied, following along with Joe as Sallie stayed with Dimar, marking their trail. "And a fire to dry our clothes. This rain will never stop!"

Snowball was completely forgotten in the excitement. He clung desperately to the limb of the tree, too frightened to descend.

Chapter 5 / Uncle Ned to the Rescue

Elizabeth and Morning Star arrived at Bird-town, hurriedly told Mandie's great uncle, Wirt Pindar, what they had come for and in no time flat they were riding toward the mountain with Wirt leading a group of men. Elizabeth insisted on going along and was given a pony to ride, but Uncle Wirt reminded her that she would have to climb the mountain on foot when they reached it.

By the time the foot of the mountain was in sight, the rain began.

"Well, looks like we're going to have a wet hike," she remarked as she dismounted. Gathering her long skirt about her, she tucked the hem into the waistband so as not to be slowed down by the weight of the wet material about her feet.

"Yes, will be hard find trail in rain," Uncle Wirt told her. He motioned for his men to come together and then gave them directions to spread out up the mountain as they climbed.

Morning Star took Elizabeth's hand and motioned toward the men. Together they followed Uncle Wirt up the incline in the downpour.

"Morning Star, pray," Elizabeth told her, clasping her hands together and looking toward the sky. She knew the Cherokees always looked up to God in the sky rather than bowing their heads when they prayed. "Pray!"

Morning Star understood and stopped to raise her face and hold her hand on her heart as she prayed in Cherokee.

"Please, God, guide and direct us to our lost children!" Elizabeth implored. "We put our faith in you!"

They quickly caught up with Wirt as he climbed through thick, wet underbrush. Morning Star was experienced in this kind of thing, while Elizabeth was hardly a match for the dense undergrowth in the pouring rain. But in her determination to find the children, she quickly adapted to the way the Indians were stepping and making their way.

"We climb opposite side. Ned climb from Deep Creek. We climb from Bird-town," Wirt explained as they kept going.

"Yes, I realize that," Elizabeth replied, pulling a brier from her skirt. "That is good; we will be covering two sides of the mountain between us."

It was a long, tedious journey up the mountainside in the heavy rain. The Indians were watchful for any sign of a trail and now and then paused to send a loud whistle through the woods in hopes of being heard by the children.

Covered with bruises and scratches, Elizabeth forced herself to keep up with Morning Star who, in spite of her age, was as agile as the men in the party. She paused only a second to catch her breath after a steep climb over boulders that were constantly in their way. She kept a prayer in her heart that no harm come to the missing ones. She had lost her twelve-year-old daughter when she was a baby and had only recently been reunited with her. Those memories kept her diligent on the path now.

Wirt, worried about the white woman trying to keep up with the Indians, called for a rest stop at the bottom of a huge boulder.

"We sit," he commanded, pointing to a clearing under a ledge projecting from the boulder above. "Rest."

"Please don't stop on my account," Elizabeth called breathlessly. "I can keep up with you."

"Sit, rest," he told her. "Morning Star need rest, too." He pointed to the old Indian woman who sat down on the rocky floor under the ledge.

Elizabeth followed her, glad for the rest. The men also came under the shelter to get out of the rain.

"While we rest, we send message," Wirt told them. Stepping back out into the rain, he gave his loud whistle that rang through the trees. Turning, he instructed the men, "You next, then you, until all give message."

The men, one at a time, stepped out and repeated the loud call through the woods. As the last one turned to sit down, there came an answering call in the distance, barely discernible through the sound of the rain.

"Ned near us. His call!" Wirt cried excitedly as he ran up the face of the boulder, whistling again. His men followed.

Morning Star and Elizabeth smiled joyfully. Maybe Uncle Ned had some good news. They lifted their skirts and ran after the men as fast as they could manage.

Uncle Ned, hearing the call and answering, turned to Uncle John as they stopped beneath a tree.

"Wirt must be near. That his call," the old Indian said.

"Someone must have let him know," Uncle John replied. Then he spoke up excitedly. "Elizabeth! Of course—she wouldn't sit there all this time and do nothing. She has rounded up our kinpeople at Bird-town."

Uncle Ned grunted and the two men, with the others following, started out in the direction from which the call had come.

It didn't take the two parties long to meet. Elizabeth ran forward as John came to meet her.

"Any word?" they both asked at once.

They both shook their heads in the negative as their arms flew around each other.

Wirt was speaking in Cherokee to Uncle Ned. Elizabeth, raising her head from John's shoulder, heard a soft meow. She looked up to see Snowball still clinging to a limb in the tree.

"Snowball!" she cried, pointing.

Everyone turned to look. John quickly scaled the tree, picked up the frightened kitten and brought it down to Elizabeth.

She stroked the wet kitten who clung to the shoulder of her dress. Her voice trembled as she spoke, "Oh, John, where can Mandie be without Snowball?"

Uncle Ned walked over to the tree. There his quick eyes caught sight of the broken branches on the bushes.

"Trail!" he said, quickly pointing to twigs jutting out at angles on the bushes ahead. "Quick! Follow trail!" He hurried ahead, watching for the marked bushes.

The two parties of searchers fell in behind him and made their way through the brush.

Meanwhile, the three children arrived at Dimar's mother's house and were welcomed in to dry by the fire and to partake of a meal. As soon as they had gotten inside the log cabin, the rain stopped.

"This is my mother, Jerusha," Dimar told them, and turning to his mother, he said, "These are friends I found lost in the woods—Mandie, Sallie, and Joe."

"Ah, my papooses," she said, hurrying to them. "Come." She took the girls by the hand and led them behind a curtain at the far end of the room. "You wrap in blanket," she said, handing them each a blanket from the beds.

Sallie explained in Cherokee that they must find the way back to her grandfather's house as soon as their clothes had dried and they had eaten.

The girls went back to the fire, and Jerusha spread their dresses to dry. Dimar helped Joe find a blanket and hung up his wet clothes.

"Now, we eat," the woman said smiling.

She brought them tin plates filled with ham, corn, and beanbread, and cups of steaming hot coffee were set on the hearth. The three ate as though they had not eaten in a week.

"Oh, how good!" Joe said, with his mouth full as he continued to cram in the food.

"This is the best meal I think I've ever had," Mandie added.

"Good food," Sallie agreed.

Dimar and his mother sat nearby, having their meal and watching the three. Jerusha kept turning the clothes so the heat would dry them.

"Eat. Much food," she told them. She rose and refilled Joe's plate but the two girls refused.

"I just can't eat anymore," Mandie told her. "I'm full up to here." She touched her throat and laughed.

"Me, too. The food was very good. We thank you." Sallie smiled as she pulled the blanket closely around her.

Even though it was summertime and terribly hot during the day, the rain cooled the air considerably. All the homes had a fire in the fireplace for cooking, and today it felt especially good.

Everyone jumped at the sound of voices outside. Mandie was the first to look out.

"It's Uncle Ned!" she cried and, securing her blanket, ran to open the door. Joe and Sallie joined her.

Uncle Ned cried with joy as he took the three into his arms. John and Elizabeth crowded in behind him.

"Uncle Ned! Mother! Uncle John!" Mandie cried excitedly.

Elizabeth handed the wet kitten to Mandie.

"Snowball! How could I not have missed you?" she said, cuddling the kitten to her blanket. She ran to the fireside and fed him the scraps on her plate, which he swallowed at once and began searching for more. Jerusha was quick to comply.

It was a joyous occasion and everyone was talking at once. Jerusha made them all feel welcome and brought out more food. The cabin was filled with so many people, there was only room to stand. Tsa'ni sulked over in a corner, afraid to mingle with the crowd. His eyes kept darting from Mandie to Sallie to Joe. Mandie ignored him. She could feel the hatred in the air between them, though she knew she shouldn't hate him. She shouldn't hate anyone. But it was so hard to be nice to an enemy. She was afraid all her Cherokee kinpeople would be like Tsa'ni and would not like her because she was mostly white.

Uncle John grabbed her hand and led her to Wirt Pindar.

"Mandie, this is your Great Uncle Wirt. He is your grandmother's youngest brother."

The old man bent to embrace her.

"My real uncle!" she exclaimed, backing off a little to look at him. He was also looking her over. "My very own uncle!"

"Jim Shaw's papoose!" the old man said softly. "Look like Jim Shaw, but have Indian thumb." He was holding her hand and examining it.

"Indian thumb?" the girl questioned him.

"Short, blunt thumb," he explained, holding his own next to hers. They were similar in shape.

"I have a Cherokee thumb!" she cried. "I'm so glad!" She turned to John. "Uncle John, let me see your thumb."

He held out his thumb and laughed. "We both have one like Uncle Wirt's."

"Little one come to Wirt's house," the old man said.

"Oh, yes, Uncle Wirt. We *are* coming to visit you," Mandie replied.

"Today," he said. "Not far to Bird-town."

Uncle Ned was standing nearby listening. "Close to Bird-town. Far to Deep Creek. We go to Bird-town."

"Now," began Elizabeth as the three gathered around her, "I want to know exactly what happened. *Where* have you been?"

Tsa'ni, wide-eyed and listening from across the room, moved in closer to hear what they would say. Mandie saw him and took pity on him. She thought, *I won't tell a lie. I just won't tell everything.*

She looked back at her mother. "We got lost in the cave and couldn't find Tsa'ni," Mandie told her.

"And we couldn't find the way we came in so we dug our way out," Joe added.

"Yes, and then those strange people in the woods tied us up and left us in the barn," Sallie explained.

"But how did you get separated from Tsa'ni?" Uncle John asked.

"Well, we stopped to look into a pool of water and I

guess it was then we got separated," Mandie replied.

Tsa'ni was holding his breath as he eavesdropped. He did not understand why the girl did not tell the whole story.

"Do not see how got lost from Tsa'ni," Uncle Ned said.

Sallie answered her grandfather. "I suppose he thought we were right behind him, but we stopped to look into the water and then we lost him."

"And how did you dig your way out of the cave?" Elizabeth wanted to know.

"Well, there was a pile of rocks and—" began Joe.

"—and a pile of gold," Mandie interrupted. "And I mean a pile of gold! And then we could see the daylight through the rocks, so we dug with our hands until we had all the rocks out of the way."

"Gold?" Uncle John asked as he looked at Uncle Ned. "You saw gold in that cave?"

Tsa'ni moved a little bit closer. They had found gold in the cave? They must be lying.

"Yes," Mandie affirmed. "It was all under the rocks we dug through to get out."

"But then the rocks all fell in and the hole closed up as soon as we got through it," Joe added.

"Do you know of any gold in that cave, Uncle Ned?" John asked.

"No. No gold. Maybe mica in rocks," Uncle Ned said.

"But it was *gold*, Uncle Ned. We saw it!" Mandie insisted, forgetting about the nugget in her pocket.

"No one goes in cave. Dangerous. Rocks fall in," the old Indian said.

"Maybe it was mica you saw, but, anyway, we're so thankful you are all safe," Elizabeth told them. "Now, don't you think we'd better get going so we can get to Uncle Wirt's house before dark?"

The three scrambled for their clothes. As Mandie put on her dress behind the curtain, the gold nugget fell out of her pocket and lay unnoticed on the floor by the bed.

Tsa'ni, breathing a sigh of relief that he was not implicated by the three, swaggered up to Mandie and said in a low voice, "You have no Indian blood in you. You could not even find your way back. You are just white, that is all."

Dimar, standing nearby, overheard and spoke up, "Tsa'ni, you are a disgrace to the Cherokees, talking like that to your own blood."

Joe advanced toward Tsa'ni. "You look here, Tsa'ni, Mandie is a well-seasoned traveler. She made a journey all the way from Almond Station to her Uncle John's house in Franklin, through the woods, across the rivers, and over the mountain. And that is rough terrain. Why, she even—"

Mandie caught him by the arm and interrupted. "Never mind, Joe. We have to go now. Come on." She turned to Sallie who was also listening. "Just ignore him."

Sallie nodded in agreement.

Wirt came over to Tsa'ni, who was his grandson. "You go to Deep Creek; bring John Shaw's things to my house. They stay with me. Make haste."

Tsa'ni looked at the old man. "I am on my way," he said. He turned and gave the three a know-it-all look and walked out the door.

Tsa'ni had no plans to do what his grandfather had asked. He had plans of his own.

Chapter 6 / Cherokee Kinpeople

Uncle Ned and his group went to Bird-town with the others. They were all tired and it was the closest place to go.

Mandie, who had ridden behind her mother on the pony from the foot of the mountain, looked around, her eyes taking in everything. This was part of the Cherokee Indian Reservation here at Bird-town. This was the original land where her Indian ancestors had lived. It was like a small town with a wide dirt road running through it. Rows of log cabins were spaced apart by crops.

There seemed to be an unusual number of women and children waiting along the road. Most of the men had gone with the search party, and they were now returning to their families.

Elizabeth followed Wirt Pindar to his house. It was the largest in the group and was in the center of the community. Aunt Saphronia, Wirt's wife, embraced them and made them welcome. She was a tiny Indian woman with a million wrinkles in her face. She had food cooked and waiting. Her neighbors, some of whom were relatives, opened their doors to the extra men from Deep Creek.

Saphronia then spotted Mandie.

"Jim Shaw's papoose!" she cried as she hugged the girl. "Love!"

"Mandie, this is your Uncle Wirt's wife, Aunt Saphronia," Elizabeth told her as John Shaw came up behind her.

"I love you, too, Aunt Saphronia," Mandie said, blinking back tears as her father's name brought back memories.

"Aunt Saphronia." John Shaw smiled as he put his arms around the little woman.

Saphronia looked up into his face. "Take care Jim Shaw's papoose."

"Yes, I will, Aunt Saphronia, together with her mother Elizabeth here," he replied.

"You forget," Elizabeth reminded him. "I have already been here. When we came to get Uncle Wirt, I met Aunt Saphronia then." She smiled at the old squaw.

"Right. I'd forgotten in all the excitement," he replied, grinning as he put one of his arms around Elizabeth and tried to include Mandie.

The girl laughed. "I don't think your arms are long enough to hug three of us at one time."

"Eat. Food ready," Saphronia told them, leading them to the table.

As they sat at the long table Mandie turned to her Uncle Wirt. "Tell me about my grandmother, Uncle Wirt, when she was a young girl. What did she look like?"

Uncle Wirt cleared his throat as he strove for the right words. "Talitha beautiful—more than others. She sing, she dance, she smile. Braves follow her. She like everyone. Everyone love her. She born here."

"She was born here?" Mandie was surprised. She had never thought about that. "Before our people were made to move out and give up their land?"

"Yes. She oldest papoose. Me youngest. All gone to happy hunting ground, but me," he said sadly.

"I love you, Uncle Wirt. I thank God that I am able to come to see my Cherokee kinpeople. He has been good to me," she said.

The old man's face brightened. He smiled. "Love, Papoose. Jim Shaw's papoose."

The others had been listening and now Uncle John spoke up.

"Talitha was my mother, you know, Mandie. But I didn't know her well because I had to go away to school as a small boy, and she was very ill. It was a long time before I had a chance to come back, but I have been back many times since then. Your father also came to visit, at least once a year, but he never knew our mother. She died not long after he was born."

"When she died our father lost all interest in life. He just pined away. He died when your father was only five years old," he said.

"Five years old," Mandie said thoughtfully. "Then you took care of my father while he was growing up."

"Yes, Jim and I lived in the house in Franklin until he got married," Uncle John said. "Uncle Ned and Morning Star lived with us for several years. He taught us both how to fish, swim, and how to use a bow and arrow."

"They lived with you and my father?" Mandie was surprised. She turned to the old Indian. "Uncle Ned, you never told me that."

Uncle Ned smiled. "Take many moons tell Papoose many things."

Dimar Walkingstick came in through the doorway and went straight to Mandie. Everyone was surprised to see him because they had left him at home with his mother when they came to Bird-town.

He held something out to Mandie. "Here. I think this is yours. It was on the floor where your dress was hung to dry."

Mandie took the gold nugget and gasped, "Oh, Dimar, thank you! I had forgotten about it entirely."

"Sit. Eat," Uncle Wirt told the boy, sliding closer to Uncle Ned to make room for him. Dimar squeezed into a place between the two old Indian men, directly facing Mandie. His eyes fastened on her and remained fixed as she showed the others what he had brought.

"You *did* take a nugget with you!" Sallie exclaimed.

"Holding out on us, huh?" Joe teased.

"You see, Uncle John," she said, handing him the nugget. "There *is* gold in the cave. It *is* gold, isn't it?"

"It certainly is," Uncle John said, passing the nugget on to the two Indian men. "Look at that!"

Uncle Ned grunted. "Cherokee not know gold in cave."

Uncle Wirt agreed. "No, Cherokee not know."

The two old men looked at each other and seemed to be concerned.

"How much do you think was there?" Uncle John asked.

"Probably a bushel basket full, wouldn't you say, Joe, Sallie?" Mandie answered.

Sallie nodded. Joe said, "Oh, probably more than that. I'd say several tote sacks full."

"Let's see, you said you found it under some rocks when you were digging a hole to get out of the cave?" Uncle John questioned.

"Yes, sir," Mandie said. "We found this pile of rocks

and could see the daylight through a tiny hole in the middle of them so we started digging to see if there was an opening. There was only a small layer of rocks over the pile of gold."

"Between the three of you, could you find the pile again?" Uncle John wanted to know.

"I don't know. You see, as soon as we got through the hole all the rocks came tumbling down from above and covered up the opening we'd dug," Mandie said.

"Unless the rockslide changed things drastically inside the cave, I think I would recognize the place," Joe added.

Uncle John turned to Sallie. "What about you, Sallie? Would you remember where it was?"

"Gold has always been back luck for the Cherokees. I would rather not look for it," the Indian girl replied.

Everyone turned to look at Sallie.

"I know what you are referring to—the removal of Indians because of the discovery of gold in Georgia. But it wouldn't be like that now," John reminded her.

Uncle Ned spoke up. "Cave dangerous. Cherokee not need gold."

"But, Uncle Ned, there must be a fortune there," John said.

"Cave not too dangerous. Tsa'ni go there many times," Uncle Wirt put in.

"That's right. Tsa'ni goes there. Has he ever found any gold?" John asked.

"No," Wirt said. "We go to cave when sun up."

"Uncle Ned, will you come with us?" John asked.

"Papoose go, Ned go. I promise Jim Shaw." He nodded his head. "But—gold bad for Cherokee."

"May I go, too?" Dimar spoke up.

Everyone had forgotten about him.

"Of course, if you want to," John told him.

Dimar rose. "I must return home now. I will meet you at the cave tomorrow morning."

So plans were made for another search—this time for a pile of gold. And this time they wouldn't get lost.

Meanwhile, Tsa'ni had gone straight to the cave from Dimar's house. He did not bother to go on to Deep Creek and deliver the Shaws' belongings to Bird-town as his grandfather had asked. He felt sure the others would return to look for the gold and he wanted to beat them to it.

He didn't have much oil left in his lantern, but he would hurry before the light went out. He knew his way around inside the cave pretty well. He hurried from one room to another, swinging the light close to the wall as he went. According to what he had heard them say, they had found the gold next to a wall.

Once, as he paused to look carefully at a pile of rocks, he thought he heard voices. He stood still and listened but could hear nothing.

"Hmm, probably the echoes of old Tsali!" he said to himself, and went on about his search.

He knew which room the bats lived in so he carefully avoided them. He was certain gold couldn't be in there anyway. They would never have stayed long enough to dig out a hole in the wall with the bats flying about their heads.

As he carefully searched tunnel after tunnel, the light in the lantern began to grow dim as the oil was being used up. He shook it and gave a sigh. He would have to leave, go home and refill the lantern before he could continue his search.

As he wound his way back toward the entrance, the

light finally sputtered and died, leaving him in total darkness. He felt his way forward slowly. As he crossed the cavern with the huge hole in the middle of the floor, he stumbled on a broken rock. Losing his balance, he grabbed desperately for the rocks, but slid back and fell directly into the pit. Just as he thought he'd never hit bottom, he landed with a splash, his head cracked against a stone, and he knew no more.

Chapter 7 / The Pit

"Are y'all ready to go prospectin'?" Joe called through the wall in the upstairs room the next morning as the rooster crowed in Uncle Wirt's yard below.

"Yep!" Mandie yelled back as she jumped out of bed and stretched. Snowball followed her.

"I will go with you," Sallie said as she rose to reach for her dress hanging on a nail.

"Beat you downstairs!" Joe called, and the girls could hear him scrambling down the ladder.

The adults were already sitting around the table. It seemed no matter how early the young ones got up, the older ones were always there first.

"I was just going to wake you," her mother said. "On this trip to the cave we are going prepared. You must eat a good breakfast, and we will carry more food. I understand we have an uphill climb on a footpath after we leave the wagon on the road, so we can't carry anything heavy."

"Besides, we have to carry lots of lanterns," Mandie told her. "It's awfully dark in that cave."

"Yes, and I have lots of rope handy, too," Uncle John added.

"Shouldn't we take something to bring the gold back in?" asked Joe as he sat down to eat beside the girls.

"Oh, yes, the men will take something to put it in—if we find it," John smiled.

"Gold—bad luck," Uncle Ned mumbled as he rose from the table.

"Hurry. We go soon," Uncle Wirt told the young people as he also stood up. "Eat."

Mandie laughed. "That's one English word my Cherokee kinpeople all know—eat." She dug into her bowl of cornmeal mush.

"Eat—that's a good word to know," Joe said.

"Do you like what our people eat? Do you eat the same thing when you are at home?" Sallie asked the two as she began eating her mush.

Mandie and Joe looked at each other.

"Well, yes, almost the same thing." Mandie paused. "Everything I have eaten since I came to Cherokee country has been delicious."

"At home we have fatback and red-eye gravy sometimes, and grits," Joe added.

Elizabeth was packing meat and bread in several separate packages. "Let's make haste now," she called. "We don't want to be too late coming back." Turning to John, she asked, "Tsa'ni never came with our things from Uncle Ned's house, did he?"

"No," he replied. "We can stop and get them on the way back."

As they went through the community at Deep Creek, they asked several people, but no one had seen Tsa'ni. They left Morning Star at her cabin and said they would stop for their things on the way back. Tsa'ni's mother was not in her cabin as they stopped by.

Uncle Ned mumbled, "Bad Cherokee."

Uncle Wirt, his grandfather, agreed, "Tsa'ni not good."

However, there was one Indian boy they could depend upon. Dimar was sitting on a rock near the waterfall waiting for them when they got there. His eyes fastened on Mandie again. He rose and came forward.

"Good morning," he greeted them.

"Good morning, Dimar," Uncle John replied. "You haven't seen Tsa'ni around, have you? He never did come to Bird-town."

"No, I have not seen him," the boy said. "I have not seen anyone around here."

"Tsa'ni—bad Cherokee," Uncle Ned muttered. "Go." He motioned for the others to follow him under the waterfall and into the cave.

"Since we aren't sure what direction to take, we'll all scatter out in different directions, but you three be sure to stay together," Uncle John told them. "Now let's all go looking for a pile of rocks!"

Elizabeth took one look at the cave and shuddered as she turned to the three children. "To think you were lost in here! I would have been frightened to death!"

"It sure wasn't any fun," Joe answered, shifting the coil of rope he was carrying over his shoulder.

"No, it wasn't." Mandie agreed.

Sallie took a lighted lantern from one of the men. "Come, we will look together." She motioned for Mandie and Joe to follow her.

"I'm glad you decided to come with us," Mandie told the Indian girl.

"Since my grandfather was coming, I decided I should try to help, too," she answered.

"Please be careful," Elizabeth warned them.

Uncle John called after them. "Yes, you be *very* careful. We don't want to have to go looking for you again."

"We will," Mandie promised as she picked up Snowball. "I think we can find it."

"Don't worry, Mrs. Shaw. We can't get lost with everyone in here," Joe said.

With Sallie leading the way with the lantern, the three went off down a tunnel. This time they were laughing, feeling very secure with the grown-ups nearby. They stopped to look at every little pile of rocks they could find along the way.

"That can't be it," Joe said as Mandie and Sallie walked over to a rock-covered wall. "The place we went through had a smooth wall all around except for the pile of stones covering the gold."

"No, Joe, it had lots of rocks stacked all along the wall," Mandie disagreed.

"Now wait a minute, Mandie. It did not!" Joe countered. Turning to the Indian girl, he asked, "Didn't it, Sallie?"

"I do not know, Joe. Do you not remember the lantern went out and we were digging in the dark?"

Mandie and Joe looked at each other.

"That's right, Sallie," he said.

"Yes, you dropped the lantern, Joe! It must be wherever you dropped it," Mandie reminded him. "We'll find the broken glass—"

"Aw, now, come on, Mandie. All those rocks fell on top of it. It's probably well buried by now," Joe interrupted.

"We have not passed the room with the bats in it

yet," Sallie said. "The bats flew at us before we found the gold."

"Oh, goodness, I had forgotten about the bats," Mandie groaned. "Do you suppose we could pass quietly so they won't get stirred up again?"

" 'Course not, Mandie. There's no way you can sneak up on bats. They are very sensitive," Joe admonished her. "We'll just have to watch out and get away fast when they come out."

They rounded a corner and a whirring, cackling noise greeted them.

"Here they come!" Sallie yelled as they bent low and ran down the passageway.

The terrifying black creatures circled and circled before they finally roosted again in their hiding place.

"Whew, that was close!" Mandie said, breathlessly, pulling Snowball's claws loose from her shoulder, "Snowball, calm down. Let go!"

"We are getting close to the place," Sallie said. "Remember, it was not long after we saw the bats that we found the opening."

"There was a large hole in the floor of that room where the gold was," Mandie reminded them. "We walked around it before coming to the pile of rocks."

"Right," Joe agreed.

Meanwhile, Uncle Ned was leading Elizabeth and John around another way. Uncle Wirt had taken Dimar with him in still another direction.

Uncle Ned pointed to cracks in the walls and ceiling and kept muttering, "Dangerous! Cave not good!"

"But Uncle Ned, these cracks look like they have been here a long, long time," John replied, examining them closely.

"Long time. Ready to fall now," the old Indian said.

"John, if this thing started caving in we'd never get out," Elizabeth fretted.

"This is a huge cave, Elizabeth, and the walls look like pretty solid rock. Even the floor is mostly rock," John said. "Anyway, we'll hurry." He put his arm around her tightly.

"John, I wonder where the children have gone," she said.

"Papooses not lost," Uncle Ned reassured her as he continued on through the tunnel they were in.

"I would like to know what happened to Tsa'ni," John remarked.

"Tsa'ni—bad Indian," Uncle Ned repeated.

They wandered on through the tunnel, searching for the pile of rocks that might be covering a pile of gold.

In another tunnel Joe was leading the way with the lantern when he yelled, "Here's the room with the hole in the floor!"

The girls joined him to look at the place. There it was —the hole in the floor of the cavern where they had found the gold.

"Now, our opening must have been over there," Joe said, pointing across to the other side.

At that moment the three heard a low moan and then a weak cry, "Help!"

They stood absolutely still with fright.

"W-w-w-wh-what was th-that?" Joe whispered.

"It may be the spirit of Tsali," Sallie replied.

"But Charlie didn't die in this cave," Joe said.

Again there was a call for help, this time a little louder.

"Sounds like it came up from that hole in the floor," Mandie said, not moving an inch.

"Who is it?" Sallie called in a loud voice.

"It is me, Tsa'ni. Please help me!" he answered, more clearly now.

Mandie was suddenly seeing another day, another call for help. She was remembering the panther and her terrible predicament. Tsa'ni had turned and left her alone. But she couldn't do that to him. No matter how mean he had been, she would have to help him now.

"Where are you, Tsa'ni?" Mandie called to him.

"I fell in the opening in the floor. I am down here at the bottom of it," the boy said.

"Tsa'ni!" Joe ventured to the edge of the hole, and swinging the lantern he could faintly see something at the bottom of the pit. "Why should we help you after what you did to us?"

Mandie hesitated, fighting with her own feelings.

"No, Joe, we must help him," she said, coming to his side.

"He must have come back here looking for our gold." Joe frowned. "He's not honest. I won't help him."

"Oh, but Joe, the Bible says we should return good for evil," Mandie reminded him. "You know that."

"Well, anyway, there's nothing we can do to help him. The hole is too deep," the boy argued.

"Are you hurt, Tsa'ni?" Sallie called down to the boy.

"Yes, I cannot move," he answered in a weak voice.

"Joe, let's tie our rope around that stalagmite over there and I'll scoot down to see what's wrong with him," Mandie suggested.

"Are you crazy? There's no telling what's down in that hole," Joe argued.

"I will help," Sallie told Mandie.

"You can't climb down a rope," Joe reprimanded.

"I can so. It's not much different than climbing a tree, and I've climbed quite a few trees in my life," Mandie said, as she put Snowball down and began to pull the end of the rope from Joe's shoulder, "Come on. Unroll the rope."

Joe set the lantern down and did as Mandie asked. They fastened the rope as tightly as they could knot it and pulled it over to the hole as Mandie prepared to descend.

"Go very slowly," Sallie warned.

Pulling up the slack in the rope, Mandie finally wriggled around on the edge of the hole so that she was swinging down. Joe held the lantern as far out as he could over the hole.

Snowball, watching Mandie slide down the rope, reached over with his paw and started to claw at it.

"Snowball, stop that!" Mandie commanded, looking up at him.

Sallie picked up the kitten. "I will hold him. He might fall."

Mandie slid on down until her feet touched the bottom. She looked around in the dim light until she saw Tsa'ni lying on his back watching her. She let go of the rope and bent over him.

"What's wrong, Tsa'ni?" she asked. "Where are you hurt?"

"I do not know. I cannot move," he said.

The girl saw a stream of water near where he lay. She took off her apron and dipped it.

"Here, let me wash your face," she said. "But I'll warn you. It's pretty cold."

She wiped his face gently and he didn't move.

"Tsa'ni, we have to figure out a way to get you out of here," she said.

"Please, go for help," he begged. "Get some strong men to help me."

"Uncle Ned and Uncle John and your grandfather are all in the cave somewhere," she told him. "You just lie still and we'll go find them. It shouldn't take very long." She dipped her apron into the water again, squeezed it out, and placed it across his forehead. "There, I'll leave that right there. Maybe it'll help. Now I'll go back up the rope and get help."

"Please hurry," the Indian boy moaned.

"We will," Mandie called back as she caught the rope. By pulling it tight and bracing her feet against the wall of the pit, she was able to work her way back up to the top. Sallie and Joe pulled her onto the floor at the top.

"Well, what's wrong with him?" Joe asked.

"He can't move, Joe. We must find the men as fast as we can."

Mandie picked up Snowball as they hurried through the tunnels and caverns calling the men's names. It was a few minutes before they finally got an answer.

"Here, Papoose. Stay there. We come," Uncle Ned called from somewhere out of sight.

"That's Amanda," Elizabeth said.

"Maybe they've found the gold," John said as they followed Uncle Ned in the direction of the voices.

Turning a sharp corner they were met by a flood of light from Mandie's lantern.

"Uncle Ned, Uncle Ned, we found Tsa'ni! He's hurt— bad. He's in a deep hole. It will take some strong men to get him out."

"Show us, Mandie," Uncle John said, and turning to Uncle Ned, he added, "So he came back here looking for the gold."

Uncle Ned nodded his head and grunted. Then he

gave his whistle for help. Uncle Wirt and Dimar were not far off and came on the run. Soon they were all in the cavern with the hole in the floor.

"There!" Mandie said, pointing. "He's down there. I went down to see what was wrong with him. He can't move."

She showed them the rope still fastened in place.

"Papoose good Indian," Uncle Ned said, putting his arm around her.

Mandie, pleased beyond expression by the compliment, looked up in his face with a big smile. "Thank you, Uncle Ned."

"This is the room where we found the gold," Joe told them. "I think it was over there where all those rocks are spilled all over the floor."

"Over there?" Uncle John was trying to distinguish the rocks he was talking about in the dim light from the lanterns.

"But first we have to get Tsa'ni out!" Mandie reminded them.

The two Indian men were already making a rope ladder to get down inside the pit.

"If he can't move, Uncle Ned, it's going to take some doing to get him out," John said, helping with the rope.

"Make basket. Put basket down hole," the old Indian replied. He was busy weaving the rope they had been carrying into a crude basket. Wirt and Dimar were helping, evidently knowing exactly what he had in mind. Uncle John finally understood. He walked around the hole to the other side, carrying the end of the rope from which they were making the basket. The other end stayed on the other side. The rope was fastened on each side to the basket so it could be lowered into the pit and then pulled back up.

Dimar volunteered. "I am young and strong. I will go down and put Tsa'ni in the basket."

"Go," Uncle Ned told him, and he slid down the rope Mandie had used.

"I am at the bottom," Dimar called. "Send down the basket."

The crude basket was lowered and Dimar pulled it flat on the rock floor of the pit. He and Tsa'ni were about the same size, and it was no easy job to lift the other boy and lay him on the rope basket. Neither spoke a word.

"All right, pull! He is in the basket," Dimar called.

The men carefully pulled on the rope from either side of the hole, and soon the basket with Tsa'ni in it appeared.

"That way," Uncle Ned motioned to the men on both sides to walk to the far end of the pit, holding the rope taut as they went. Then they lowered the basket carefully to the floor. Uncle Wirt bent to examine the injured boy.

"I cannot move," Tsa'ni told his grandfather. His face was pale and he looked frightened in the lantern light.

"We take Tsa'ni to wagon," Wirt told the others.

Tsa'ni turned his head away.

Joe protested as they prepared to leave. "What about the gold?"

"We'll have to use the wagon to get Tsa'ni to a doctor. We'll just have to come back tomorrow," Uncle John told them.

Mandie sighed. "Oh, me. All this work all over again." She was feeling hatred again toward Tsa'ni for interfering with their plans. After all, he had fallen into the pit because he was trying to beat them to the gold.

"Yeh, all because of that stupid boy," Joe said.

Sallie looked at the two, "He will be sorry."

"I hope he is," Joe said. "First thing you know,

someone else will get the gold, and we'll never know what happened to it. So many people know about it now."

Mandie and Sallie agreed. Too many people knew about the gold. They must hurry back the next day.

Chapter 8 / The Broken Wagon Wheel

Uncle Ned pulled the wagon to a halt in front of his cabin and motioned to the others. "Wirt and me take Tsa'ni to doctor. You stay here. Morning Star make food."

"Are you sure you won't need any help?" Uncle John asked as he helped Elizabeth down from the wagon. "No. You watch papooses," Uncle Ned said, laughing.

"I don't think they'll go anywhere. It's past suppertime and I know they're hungry," Uncle John told him.

Mandie, Joe, Sallie, and Dimar jumped down and headed for the cabin. Dimar had told his mother he would be gone for a day or two, so he decided to stay at Uncle Ned's house for the night.

Morning Star had the food cooking and Elizabeth helped her finish. The four young people sat on the doorstep with Snowball.

"Where are they taking Tsa'ni to a doctor?" Mandie asked Sallie.

"To Dr. Carnes. He is a white doctor. He lives between here and Bryson City," the Indian girl replied.

"He probably won't find anything wrong with him. I

think it's all put on so he won't get into trouble for trying to steal the gold," Joe remarked, as he drew lines in the sand with a stick.

"But, Joe, he didn't say a word all the way back. He had his eyes closed," Mandie said, secretly thinking the same thing as Joe. She was desperately trying to rid her mind of the mean thoughts.

"Well, I could do that, too. Saves answering a whole lot of questions," Joe chided.

"I do not think so, Joe," Sallie disagreed. "I really believe he was hurt. He looked pale and weak."

"Well, he sure slowed things down for us."

"You're right there, Joe," Mandie said.

"Your uncle said we would return tomorrow," Dimar reminded her. His eyes never left her face. His admiration was plain to see, but Mandie was not aware of it.

"But, Dimar, we have to go all the way back up there to the cave and then all through those spooky rooms until we find the right one again," Mandie said.

"That will not be hard this time. I think I can remember exactly which way we went." Sallie was confident.

"Yeh, like that." Joe drew a rough diagram of the cave in the sand. "Here's the entrance, and we went this way." He pointed. "Then this way and that way." He sketched a line through the outline.

"That is right." Sallie was watching.

"But there's still the problem of actually finding the gold. It's buried somewhere under all those rocks, and they all look the same," Mandie reminded them.

"That should not take long with so many people to help dig," Dimar said.

Elizabeth came to the doorway. "Eat!" She laughed.

"Eat! That word is good in any language!" Joe exclaimed as they stood up and hurried to the table for their evening meal.

"Amen!" agreed Mandie.

Dimar managed to sit between Mandie and Sallie with Joe on the other side of Mandie. Joe was beginning to notice Dimar's behavior around his friend. He didn't say anything, but kept a watch on the two of them during the meal. Mandie still did not seem to notice the extra attention.

Uncle Ned returned after a while, alone. Everyone looked up, anxious for news of Tsa'ni.

"Tsa'ni go home. Wirt go with him," the old Indian told them as he sat down to eat. "Doctor say—stay in bed."

"Well, did he think it was serious? I mean, can Tsa'ni move now?" Uncle John asked.

"No," the old man replied. "Hurt back, legs."

"Well, I hope he doesn't have a *bad* back injury. He may never walk again," Elizabeth said.

Everyone became serious. Mandie was fighting elation over the fact that Tsa'ni really was injured. In the back of her mind she knew she should feel sorry for him. But she couldn't help feeling he deserved it.

She spoke up to clear her thoughts. "Can we go to see him tomorrow?"

The old Indian nodded. "Yes—Tsa'ni bad Cherokee."

"You mean because he tried to get the gold?" asked Joe.

The old man nodded again. "Gold bad for Cherokee. Tsa'ni bad, too."

Mandie turned to her Uncle John. "Are you still going back to the cave tomorrow?"

He turned to Uncle Ned. "What do you think? Should

we go back up there tomorrow?"

"Go tomorrow. Be done!" the Indian grunted.

Uncle John laughed. "You still aren't happy about looking for the gold. Uncle Ned, the Cherokees could use the gold for a lot of things they need—a hospital, a school closer by, even a new church. Depending on how much is there, the gold could buy lots of things which would take years and years to get otherwise."

"Gold make people crazy. Bad for Cherokee. Bad for Tsa'ni." He was very firm about it.

"I know, but we'll see what good we can do with it," John continued.

"You mean we can't *keep* the gold?" Joe asked, surprised at the conversation between the two men.

"Of course not, Joe," Uncle John told him. "This is Cherokee territory, so it rightfully belongs to them."

"But the cave is not on the Cherokee reservation," Joe argued.

"I know that, but it's almost one hundred percent Cherokee territory around here. Besides, that cave belongs to their history. Remember, Tsali hid in there," John added.

"Couldn't we just keep a little sample for a souvenir?" Mandie ventured.

"Depends on how big the sample is," Uncle John laughed. "Anyhow, we'll cross that bridge when we come to it."

Morning Star had been sitting at the table listening to the conversation. No one had any idea how much she had understood until she spoke up with great conviction, "Jim Shaw's papoose have gold!"

Everyone turned to look at her, startled.

She tried to explain. She pointed to herself and then

to Mandie. "My gold Papoose's gold."

Mandie jumped up to hug her. "Oh, Morning Star, you are learning to speak English! I wouldn't take your gold. Like Uncle John says, it belongs to the Cherokees living around here."

Morning Star shook her head furiously and rattled off something in Cherokee. Uncle Ned listened and turned to explain.

"Morning Star say gold bad for Cherokee. Morning Star remember Cherokee move. I remember, too."

"Times have changed, Uncle Ned," John insisted. "I can guarantee you no harm will come to the Cherokees when the gold is found. It won't be like it was before."

The old man grunted and got up to go outside. John followed him.

"Early to bed early to rise," Elizabeth told the children.

The four went to bed early, but there was a great deal of talking going on over the wall. Dimar and Joe were on the one side and the girls on the other. Joe, knowing the Indian boy was interested in Mandie, tried to monopolize the conversation.

"Mandie, this is even more exciting than looking for your uncle's will, don't you think?" Joe began.

"Well, I don't know about that," she said. "I suppose it is just *as* exciting. Of course, I've never seen so much gold before."

"Neither have I," Sallie put in.

"I sure hope we find it," Dimar said. "There must be a pile of it if it can buy a hospital and all that other stuff your Uncle John was talking about, Mandie."

"A *huge* pile of it. I have no idea how much it's worth, though," said Mandie.

"Your uncle will know," Dimar assured her.

"I'm sure glad he's around to handle everything because Uncle Ned is certainly not interested," she said.

"He can remember the removal," Dimar reminded her.

Joe, becoming jealous of the boy, faked a yawn and said loudly, "Well, time to go to sleep. Have to get up early."

"Yes, we have to get up early," Sallie agreed.

"I almost forgot something. If we are leaving early in the morning for the cave, how are we going to see Tsa'ni?" Mandie asked.

"Well, I have no intention of going to see Tsa'ni. You will just have to wait until we come back if you insist on visiting him," Joe replied.

The question was settled at early dawn when the four, wide awake with excitement, went downstairs for breakfast. Uncle Ned and Uncle John were just coming in the door from outside. They looked disturbed.

Seeing the four youngsters at the table, Uncle John explained, "Well, it looks like we won't be going back to the cave today. The wagon has a broken wheel and we have to get the part from Bryson City, which is going to take some time."

The four spoke as one, "Oh, no!"

"It wasn't broken when you came home last night, was it, Uncle Ned?" Mandie asked.

The old man shook his head. "Broke today."

Uncle John explained. "No, it wasn't broken last night. It looks like someone has been prowling around and deliberately damaged the wheel."

The four looked at one another.

"Well, since Tsa'ni can't walk, it couldn't have been him this time," Mandie said.

"How about the old man and woman that captured us in the woods?" Joe asked

"Snuff and Rennie Lou?" Mandie asked.

"Yeh, maybe it was them."

"I hardly think they would come down here and do a thing like that," Uncle John said.

"You said you told them you were going to report them to the authorities," Sallie reminded him.

"Yes, as a matter of fact, I did tell them that."

"But why would they want to do something like that?" Uncle John added.

"Maybe they know about the gold," Dimar suggested.

"And maybe they know we are going after it," added Mandie.

"Well, anyway, however it happened, we will have to wait until the wagon is repaired," John Shaw said.

"Couldn't we borrow a wagon from one of the neighbors? After all, Uncle Ned knows all of them," Mandie said.

"No, we'd rather not do that. We'd have to keep it all day, and we'd have to explain where we were going. Uncle Ned and I are going to ride into Bryson City when we get the horses saddled up and see what we can get to fix the wheel."

"Are you going to talk to the authorities about the old man and woman?" Joe asked.

"I suppose we'll do that while we're there," John said.

"They must have a still up there. Remember, we told you they thought we were spying on their still." Mandie added.

"I remember."

"May we go visit Tsa'ni while Uncle John is gone, Mother?" Mandie asked Elizabeth.

"If you want to, but you mustn't stay too long. Tsa'ni is probably too sick to be bothered with company," her mother told her.

As the men rode away to Bryson City, the four waved good-bye from the front of the cabin.

"Anyone want to go see Tsa'ni now?" Mandie asked.

"I will go with you," Sallie replied.

"I don't know. I think he is dishonest with us," Joe mumbled.

"I will go," Dimar said, eager for the chance to be with Mandie.

Joe was quick to notice, and he thought he'd better go along just to keep an eye on the two. He shuffled his feet around in the sand and looked up. "All right. I'll go, too, but I won't have anything to say to him."

Tsa'ni lived about a mile down the road from Uncle Ned's house, but the road had such a sharp curve that it was easier to cut through the backyards of several neighbors. Mandie had already decided that all the Cherokees' cabins were alike and so she was not surprised to find Tsa'ni's home a duplicate of Uncle Ned's. The door of the log cabin was open and as they approached, a kind Indian woman came to welcome them.

"Come in. I am glad you could come to see Tsa'ni," she said, as they entered the house.

The boy was on a bed at the far end of the room, and Mandie could feel him staring at her.

"I am Amanda Shaw, and you must be Tsa'ni's mother," Mandie introduced herself.

"Yes, I am Meli," the woman said. "Your father was my husband's cousin."

Mandie nodded. "That's right. How is Tsa'ni today?"

"Not good. But, go—see," she said, directing the four over to the bed.

Tsa'ni stared but did not speak.

"We came to see how you are," Mandie spoke cheer-
fully.

There was no answer.

"What did Dr. Carnes tell you about your injuries?"
she asked.

Tsa'ni seemed determined not to speak.

"You could at least answer," Dimar told him. "You
are being rude."

Tsa'ni took a deep breath. "Why should I speak to
the white girl? White people! They are always causing
trouble for the Cherokee!"

"No one caused trouble for you, Tsa'ni," Dimar re-
torted. "What happened to you was your own fault. And
you *were* rescued because Mandie cared about what
happened to you."

"The white people come here poking into the Cherokees' affairs," Tsa'ni said. "I do not want to see any more
white people!" He turned his face toward the wall.

"You are a very narrow-minded person, Tsa'ni," Mandie told him.

"Tsa'ni, if you had not been trying to find the gold
first, you would not have been injured," the Indian girl
said.

"Go away! I do not wish to communicate with white
people! I do not wish to have any company!" He still kept
his face turned away from them.

Joe was filled with anger. "You may not wish to communicate with white people, but you must admit you
tried to get the gold which we found first."

"The gold belongs to the Cherokees, not the white
people!" Tsa'ni turned to glare at Joe.

"We found it and we will do what we please with it!"
Joe insisted.

"Do not be too sure about that! Now, get out!" Tsa'ni yelled, flushed with anger.

The four backed off to leave. They stopped to say good-bye to his mother who had been watching the whole scene.

As they walked back through the yards to Uncle Ned's house, Mandie asked, "I wonder what he meant when he said we shouldn't be too sure about doing what we please with the gold?"

"Just talking," said Joe. "He wants to frighten us away from it."

"He could have told someone else about the gold," Sallie suggested.

"Yes, and they could be looking for it right now," Dimar added.

"I hope not," Mandie said. "You all heard what Uncle John said could be done with the gold, and I sure hope the wrong people don't get it."

They all felt their plans were strangely threatened. Mandie hated Tsa'ni more that ever in spite of her intentions to forget the wrongs he had done them. He was such a revengeful person. How could anyone like him?

Chapter 9 / Tsali's Message

Uncle Ned and Uncle John were back from Bryson City in time for the noontime meal. As they all sat around the table, they discussed their journey.

"Did you get the piece to fix the wagon?" Mandie asked before anyone had eaten a bite.

"Yes, as soon as we finish eating, we'll get it back in working order, and tomorrow we'll go back to the cave," Uncle John told her.

The four looked at one another and smiled.

"Eat," Uncle Ned commanded.

"Yes, sir, Uncle Ned," Mandie replied, picking up her fork, and starting on the beans. The other three followed suit.

Elizabeth turned to John. "Did you talk to anyone about those two people up in the mountain?"

"The old man and woman? Yes, we told everything we knew about them. There will be men scouting the mountain looking for a still in a few days," he said.

"We went to see Tsa'ni and he was rude to us," Mandie said. She related the conversation between them. Uncle Ned listened closely.

"Tsa'ni bad Cherokee," he mumbled. "Up to no good."

"Bad," echoed Morning Star.

"Well, there's nothing he can do if he can't get about," Uncle John told them.

"I don't trust him at all," Joe said. "I think if he *could* walk, he wouldn't let us know it."

"Joe!" Elizabeth admonished him.

"Sorry, Mrs. Shaw, but I don't trust him," Joe told her.

"I don't either, Mother," Mandie said. She had decided to give up believing the Indian boy.

"I cannot trust him either," Sallie added.

"Neither can I," Dimar joined in.

"Well, in that case, maybe there *is* some reason not to trust him," Elizabeth replied.

"Reason—Tsa'ni bad," the old Indian repeated.

"Oh, Uncle Ned, you've been saying Tsa'ni is bad ever since we got here. How about telling me why you say that?" John asked Ned.

"Leave Papoose with panther. Try to steal gold. No bring things to Bird-town," the old man explained. He took a deep breath. "Now he make bad talk to Papoose."

"The Bible says repay evil with good, remember, Uncle Ned?" John reminded him.

"Big Book not say Tsa'ni can be bad Indian," the old Indian muttered.

Everyone smiled.

Mandie couldn't understand why one should keep on doing good to a person who kept on doing bad things in return. She was quite exasperated and was losing her determination to be kind. Then she remembered her father had taught her to pray for her enemies, so she decided she would start praying for Tsa'ni. In the meantime, she hoped he would recover from his accident—but not in time to beat them to the gold!

Uncle Wirt went with them the next morning to the cave. He was still angry with his grandson and would not talk about him. He had gone on to his house in Bird-town the day before and had not seen Tsa'ni since.

After arriving inside the cave, Sallie led them straight to the cavern where they had seen the gold.

"Here is the place," she told them, pointing to the pile of rocks along the far wall.

Mandie agreed. "Yes, this is it."

"Well, let's start digging," Joe said, pushing up his sleeves.

With the three men to help them, it didn't take long to move the piles. Elizabeth watched from a safe distance as they threw the rocks behind them out of the way. Sallie found the first nugget.

"Gold," she said, handing the nugget to Uncle Ned who was working beside her.

He turned it over in his hand, didn't say a word and passed it on to John. The others crowded around.

"The real thing," John Shaw said. "Let's see how much we can find."

Mandie and Joe were moving the rocks at the bottom of the pile when she stooped and squealed. "Here it is! All of it!" They had uncovered the gold they had found before.

"At last!" Joe gasped.

The men bent to inspect the gold.

"You were right, Mandie. It is about a bushel," her uncle told her. "Now let's get it into these sacks and get out of here."

Everyone was stuffing the sacks with the gold when

Sallie, cleaning off the floor under one end of the pile, called out, "Look! Writing!" She was pointing to the wall of the cave behind the rocks.

The group gathered to see what she had found. They all worked to clean the wall and the rest of the writing. Soon large Indian sign language appeared and also some words in English.

Sallie bent close to read it. "This gold left here for good of Cherokee after white man makes peace. This gold belongs to us who are hiding here to save our lives. Curse on the white man who takes it. Tsali." She gasped as she finished the words.

All were speechless as they stared at the crude letters on the stone wall.

Joe turned to Ned. "Could it really have been Tsali who wrote this message and left the gold?"

The old Indian nodded. "His name." He pointed to the symbol under the English "Tsali."

"He did not forget his people," Dimar said very solemnly. "He gave his life and left them a fortune."

"After all these years!" Mandie exclaimed. "And to think we were the ones who discovered it!"

"Someone else must have written the message for him," Uncle John said.

"Probably the white man, William H. Thomas, who came to ask him to surrender to save his people," Sallie added. "He was the trusted friend of the Cherokee people."

"Of course," Uncle John agreed.

"Would it be possible to take the message, too, with the gold?" Mandie asked.

"You don't mean that?" Joe laughed. "That's a stone wall."

"I just don't know. I suppose we could get somebody to look at it to see if the piece of stone could be chiseled out," Uncle John suggested.

Elizabeth asked, "Wouldn't it be better to leave it here for history's sake?"

"Well—" began John.

"On, no, Mother," Mandie protested. "You see, the wall caved in on us when we climbed through the hole we dug, and sooner or later rockslides will completely cover it again and maybe even break it up. Besides, we don't want to spread word about the gold yet, do we?"

"You're right," her uncle said. "We'll see about getting it chiseled out."

"We take message out," Uncle Ned told them.

Wirt nodded.

"Please, could I help?" Dimar asked.

Uncle Ned nodded. "Strong brave."

"Let's hurry," Uncle John said, bending to help fill the sacks. "We want to get back before sundown. Uncle Ned, you and Uncle Wirt can come back whenever you get ready and see what you can do about cutting out the message."

Carefully sorting through the rocks to be sure they got it all, they finally finished filling the sacks and carried them to the wagon. It was time-consuming and back-breaking work, but it seemed worth the effort. With all this gold the Cherokees could accomplish a lot.

As they prepared to return to Uncle Ned's cabin, Uncle John warned them, "It's better that we don't discuss this with anyone outside our little group here until we can come to some decision as to how to give this gold to the Cherokee people."

Uncle Ned looked fiercely at the others. "No talk!"

Uncle Wirt added, "No talk."

The others agreed. Some plan would have to be made for distributing the gold to the Indians, and until something was finalized, it would be safer not to let anyone else know about what they had found.

It was dark when they arrived at Uncle Ned's cabin. Morning Star had the table set with food to greet them. They hurriedly unloaded the gold in the barn and covered it with hay.

"Should be safe here until we can decide something further," Uncle John said as they shut the door. He took the nail hanging on a leather strap and dropped it into the hook, the only way there was to secure the door.

They were all happy as they walked toward the cabin, not realizing they were being watched in the darkness.

Chapter 10 / Thieves in the Night

The four young people were talkative and restless long after they had gone to bed. Snowball sensed their mood and bounced around between them. There was a small window next to Mandie's bed, and she and Sallie kept peering out at the barn.

"Just think what's in the barn!" Mandie exclaimed.

"Yes, and think of how much fun it will be giving it to the Cherokees," Joe called over the dividing wall.

"It is such a dark night. If the moon were only shining, we could see the barn more clearly," the Indian girl said.

"I do not think we need to stay up all night watching the barn," Dimar said from the small room he occupied with Joe.

Sallie tensed up suddenly. "Mandie! Look! Is that someone out there?"

Mandie pressed her face against the windowpane. "Where, Sallie?"

"At the corner. There!" Sallie poked at the window.

"I can't see anyone, Sallie," Mandie was getting excited.

"Oh, I suppose it was just my imagination," Sallie admitted. "We should go to sleep."

"I can't believe those girls," Joe sighed.

"Hey, wait, I see a light! Look!" Mandie shouted.

The two girls stared hard into the darkness. Then gradually the light grew stronger.

"It's a fire! The barn is on fire!" Mandie screamed. She ran to the ladder and screamed again. "Uncle Ned, Uncle John, the barn is on fire!"

Dimar and Joe hastily pulled on their trousers and ran to see. They took one look through the window and flew down the ladder. The girls, pulling their dresses on over their heads, followed, Snowball close behind.

Uncle Ned and Uncle John were already out the door by the time the boys' feet hit the floor. Elizabeth and Morning Star were getting dressed.

"Bell!" shouted Uncle Ned to Dimar as he ran. The boy understood and ran to the huge iron bell hanging in the tree and pulled the rope. The clapper sent out a loud gong and in seconds neighboring Indians began appearing from all directions carrying water buckets.

"Oh, please, dear God, don't let it burn up!" Mandie prayed as she was held back by her mother.

There were so many men fighting the fire that it was soon extinguished with little damage done, thanks to the girls who had seen it start. Uncle Wirt had gone to his son's house for the night, and he was among the firefighters who had answered the call of the bell.

The volunteers all went home and Uncle Ned, Uncle Wirt and Uncle John stood surveying the damage.

"Thank goodness we caught it in time," John said. "That was deliberately set. I just hope whoever it was doesn't come back tonight."

"I will guard the barn," Dimar offered as he stepped forward. "I will stay out here."

Joe, not to be outdone, spoke up, "I'll help you. One of us can sleep inside while the other one watches and then we can switch."

So it was agreed. The boys stood watch for the rest of the night. The girls, more restless than ever, kept watching at the window.

"Who do you suppose set that fire?" Mandie asked as they lay by the window.

"I do not know," the Indian girl said. "But whoever it was I wish we could catch him."

"I have a feeling whoever did it knew about the gold," Mandie said.

"Yes, I think so, too," Sallie agreed.

"Tomorrow Uncle John will repair the barn and Uncle Ned and Uncle Wirt will go back and start work on chiseling out the message in the cave. And when they get done, we can do something with the gold. Uncle John said they wanted the message to show the people when they present the gold to them."

"That will be a great day for the Cherokee!" the Indian girl said.

Tired and worn out, the two girls were soon asleep in spite of their excitement. But while they slept peacefully, things were not so peaceful in Uncle Ned's yard.

Joe was trying to sleep inside on the haystack, while Dimar was on guard outside the barn. He couldn't get comfortable, his ears attuned for intruders. Finally he gave up trying to sleep and went outside to join Dimar.

"I might as well forget it," he told the Indian boy. "I can't go to sleep in there."

"I can't sleep either," Dimar said.

"How about if you stay in the front here and I'll stay at the back?" Joe asked.

"All right. Sounds good to me." Dimar was too tired to argue.

Joe walked around to the back and stretched out in the grass. He had been lying there for what seemed like hours to him, when he heard the soft snap of a twig. He didn't move, but his ears perked up to listen. The night was so dark it was impossible to see very far. Then he heard another pop in the underbrush behind the barn. Now he was certain someone was there. He waited, his heart pounding furiously. Whoever it was, he must be out of sight lying in the tall grass.

Quietly turning on his side with his eyes trained on the brush in front of him, Joe finally distinguished the figure of a man. He took one step forward, pausing to listen, took another, then paused again. Joe waited until he was almost within reach, then bolted upright.

He could hardly believe his eyes, "Tsa'ni! You liar! You're supposed to be in bed!"

Tsa'ni stared in surprise at the sudden outburst. As he turned to run, Dimar, having heard the commotion, joined the chase. He was as surprised as Joe to see Tsa'ni.

"Tsa'ni! You are a disgrace to our people!" Dimar shouted at the fleeing Indian, who, knowing the area so well, was soon far from the reach of his pursuers.

The two boys finally gave up the chase. "Looks like we lost him," Joe said, exhausted and gasping for air.

"Yes, but now we know who started the fire, don't you think, Joe?" Dimar replied, wiping the perspiration from his forehead.

"Shall we wake up his mother and Uncle Wirt and tell them?" Joe asked. "We must be somewhere near his house. I'm sure he's the culprit all right."

"No, I think it best we wait until daylight. We can keep watch until morning, and then we'll tell Uncle Ned," the Indian boy said.

"Yeh, Uncle Ned will know what to do," Joe agreed, as they returned to the barn.

In spite of their good intentions, they both fell fast asleep and didn't awaken until daybreak, when they heard Morning Star open the door of the cabin.

They waited until everyone was gathered around the table, and then relayed the excitement of the night before.

"Uncle Ned, we think we know who set fire to your barn," Joe told the old man.

Every head turned in his directon. Just then, Uncle Wirt came in through the open door, unnoticed.

"Who?" Uncle Ned asked.

"Tsa'ni," Joe replied.

Uncle Wirt stopped in his tracks, his presence still undetected.

"Tsa'ni?" Uncle Ned repeated, shaking his head. There were a few seconds of shocked silence; then the questions began.

"How do you know, Joe?" Uncle John asked.

"We caught him prowling around the barn last night, only he escaped," Joe said.

"Joe caught him by surprise. We know it was Tsa'ni. We chased him a long time," Dimar added.

Uncle Wirt stepped forward to the table and everyone noticed him for the first time.

"Tsa'ni?" Uncle Wirt asked incredulously.

"Yes, Uncle Wirt," Joe replied.

"Tsa'ni—gone last night," Uncle Wirt nodded.

"I'm sorry, Uncle Wirt. I know he's your grandson," Uncle John sympathized.

"No. Tsa'ni bad Indian," Uncle Wirt affirmed. "He make lies."

"We chased him all through the woods, but he didn't go home," Joe said.

"But, we didn't actually *see* him set fire to the barn," Mandie spoke up. "We couldn't say for sure that he was the one who did it unless we actually saw him, right?"

"You are absolutely right, my dear," Uncle John agreed. "We are jumping to conclusions. Just because Joe and Dimar saw him near the barn last night doesn't mean he was the one who started the fire."

"But what other reason would he have for lying about not being able to walk and then showing up at Uncle Ned's barn the night of the fire?" Joe argued. "If he were just curious, he wouldn't have taken off like the wind when he saw us."

"'Judge not, lest ye be judged,'" Mandie quoted. "Do you remember our Sunday school lesson not long ago, Joe?"

Elizabeth gazed admiringly at her daughter and smiled.

"I don't understand why you are always defending him, Mandie, after all the things he has done to us." Joe shook his head.

Uncle Ned pushed a plate of food toward Uncle Wirt. "Sit. Eat. We go get message in cave."

Uncle Wirt sat down and began eating.

"I would like to talk to Tsa'ni if anybody sees him," Uncle John said.

"No one is going to be seeing him around for a while. I'm sure of that!" Joe was emphatic.

"You boys better get some sleep," Uncle John told them.

"Sleep? We want to help fix the barn!" Joe said between mouthfuls.

"Sure thing," Dimar added.

"All right, but you must both be terribly tired—or did you sleep some last night?" He looked at the boys with a knowing grin.

They both dropped their heads. Joe told him, "I guess I dozed off a little after we lost Tsa'ni."

"So did I," Dimar admitted.

Uncle Ned got his tools from the barn, harnessed up the horses to the wagon, and he and Uncle Wirt set out for the cave.

The boys went out to work on the barn with Uncle John.

Mandie and Sallie helped Morning Star and Elizabeth with chores around the house. Everyone was occupied for the day, though constantly on the alert. But just as Joe predicted, the day passed peacefully with no sign of Tsa'ni.

Inside the cave Uncle Ned and Uncle Wirt began hammering away at the stone wall. After hours and hours of work, they had made a continuous crack around the carved message and stood back to survey their work. Then there was a soft rumble. The two men held their breath listening. The rumble became louder and louder until the whole cave seemed to tremble.

"Rockslide!" gasped Uncle Ned, snatching his lantern and tools as he stumbled backward to the other side of the cavern.

The two men were temporarily stunned, and then suddenly the whole wall broke into pieces and a portion of the ceiling came crashing down. They ran for their lives. The noise was deafening. They had barely reached the entrance when the whole cave seemed to collapse. They ran without stopping until they were safely on the road. When they gazed back, it seemed the entire mountainside had changed in appearance. Huge boulders had slid down the side, dragging trees and brush with them into the waterfall. Everything in view was in shambles.

"Cave—gone!" Uncle Ned gasped.

"Gone!" echoed Uncle Wirt.

"Tsali message gone!" Uncle Ned wiped tears from his eyes as he thought about the great Indian hero who had remembered his people even in death.

Uncle Wirt could not speak. He simply turned toward the wagon on the road. Uncle Ned followed him and together they rode silently back to tell the others the news.

It was late afternoon when Mandie and Sallie saw them coming and ran to meet them. The girls could tell immediately that something was wrong.

"Uncle Ned, what happened?" Mandie asked as he stopped the wagon in front of the barn and stepped down. John and the boys came out at once.

"Cave gone. Tsali message gone," Uncle Ned shook his head in sorrow.

"Gone? How could it be gone?" Mandie asked.

"Rockslide. Cave gone. Message buried," Uncle Ned replied.

"A rockslide? Are you all right?" Uncle John asked, checking them over. "How did you manage to get out?"

"Run. God with us," Uncle Ned explained.

"Cave gone," Uncle Wirt repeated, shaking his head in bewilderment.

"That message Tsali left would have meant so much to our people," Sallie stated sadly.

"Now no one will ever believe us when we tell them about it," Joe said dejectedly.

"Part of our history has been lost," Dimar added.

"But we still have the gold," Mandie reminded them.

"Yes, and we still must decide what to do with it," Uncle John said.

As they sat around the table for the evening meal, they discussed the matter at length.

"I'll watch the barn again tonight," Joe offered after a lull in the discussion.

"So will I," Dimar said.

"You boys need a good night's rest," Uncle John told them.

"We can take our blankets and roll up in them on the grass outside. If anyone comes around, we will surely wake up," Joe insisted. Dimar nodded in agreement.

"Well, I certainly hope so," Elizabeth said. "It could be dangerous."

"Gold bad luck," Uncle Ned muttered.

"Not the gold, Uncle Ned. It's the greedy people," Mandie said.

Elizabeth spoke up. "What *are* we going to do about the gold? We can't keep it here forever."

"I know," Uncle John replied. "We'll have to decide what to do very soon."

"Why can't we put the gold in the bank?" Mandie asked.

"Good idea! Have you ever heard of bank robbers, Mandie?" Joe protested sarcastically.

"Bank robbers don't ever come to Bryson City." Mandie was sure of herself.

"I suppose the bank *is* a possible solution," John

said. Turning to Wirt and Ned, he asked, "Do you think we could get it to the bank early tomorrow morning before the town is stirring?"

Both the old men nodded affirmatively.

"Well, if the people decide to storm the bank and take it, it belongs to them anyway," Joe conceded.

"No. Gold bad luck to Cherokee," Uncle Ned insisted. "Cherokee not steal gold."

"But what about Tsa'ni?" Dimar asked. "He wanted the gold."

"Tsa'ni!" Uncle Wirt spat out. "Bad Cherokee!" He rose to leave.

"Don't be too hard on him, Uncle Wirt," Elizabeth told him. "We don't know for sure who set fire to the barn."

But Uncle Wirt was angry, it was plain to see.

"He lied about not being able to walk and he should be punished for that," John said. "Will you be back tomorrow to help us move the gold to the bank?"

"Early tomorrow," the old man nodded as he waved good-bye.

As darkness began to fall, the two boys took their blankets to spread on the grass by the barn. The girls went up the ladder to their room and watched from the window until they were too sleepy to stay awake any longer. Snowball curled up contentedly at Mandie's feet.

It was long after midnight and both boys were sleeping soundly. The figure of a man appeared out of the brush and came stealthily toward the barn. He stopped at the corner of the building and lowered the flame of his lantern to the grass against the wall.

Joe stirred uneasily in his sleep, unseen by the intruder. Then his subconscious registered the distinct odor of burning grass mixed with the stench of liquor. He was awake in a flash, taxing his brain to orient himself to the situation. Then he saw the blaze not ten feet away, and he lunged to his feet. The figure, still not aware of Joe, darted around the corner. Joe headed the other way to alert Dimar who was already awake.

"He's on that side of the barn," Joe whispered softly, pointing to the north side.

They crept around the building in opposite directions and were both surprised to find themselves face to face with Snuff and Rennie Lou. With one fell swoop Joe had Snuff on the ground. Dimar kept his eyes on Rennie Lou, who stood there in a daze.

"We got you this time!" Joe shouted as he held him to the ground.

"Hey, wait a minute. I ain't done nothin'," the man protested, his speech slurred.

Dimar took a deep breath and gave his loud Indian call for help. Within seconds Uncle John and Uncle Ned came rushing out of the cabin.

Noise of the scuffling woke the girls and they slid down the ladder and watched at the door.

"Why, it's the man and woman who captured us on the mountain," Mandie said, as she watched Uncle John "handcuff" Snuff with his belt.

Morning Star slipped past the girls without a word and joined the others outside. Rennie Lou had come out of her stupor and saw a chance for escape while Dimar and Joe went to stomp out the fire. But she was no match for the strong Indian woman, who subdued her after a short struggle.

"I ain't done nothin'!" the woman was yelling. "Leave me alone, squaw!"

Morning Star ignored her threats and kept a firm grip on her arm.

"Hey, you're a white man," she directed to Uncle John. "You gonna let this Injun woman bully me?"

"Anything she wants to do to you will be all right with me," Uncle John replied. "Don't you realize these young people are the ones you kidnapped on the mountain? You two are going to jail as soon as we can get the law to take over."

"Take palefaces to Bryson City," Uncle Ned said as he went to hitch the wagon.

"This time of night, Uncle Ned?" Elizabeth asked as she joined John.

"Yes," the old man nodded.

"He's right, Elizabeth. We can't keep them here, and they should have been behind bars before now," John told her.

"Please, mister, don't do that," Snuff begged.

Uncle John ignored him as he called to the girls, "Mandie, can you bring us some rope? We need to secure these two for the trip to town."

Sallie and Mandie came out with several coils of rope. The boys helped Uncle John tie the couple up and get them into the wagon.

"Could we go along, Uncle John?" Joe asked.

"Oh, yes, please!" Dimar joined in.

Uncle John hesitated but then added, "Well, I suppose we do need you two as witnesses of the kidnapping and the arson."

"Right!" the boys exclaimed together.

"What about us?" Mandie protested.

"This is man's work, child," Uncle John told her. And they were off.

"Mmm, so it wasn't Tsa'ni after all," Mandie said as they walked back to the house.

"No, I do not think he was the one, Mandie, and I am glad it was not a Cherokee," Sallie said.

"But he was prowling around here for some reason —probably knew we had the gold." Mandie continued. "Tsa'ni really is strange, pretending to be hurt when he isn't. I wonder if he ever went back home."

Tsa'ni had never reached home. He was at that moment caught in an abandoned hunter's trap in the woods. This time he was really hurt.

Chapter 11 / Spreading the Word

"Well, we might as well all go back to bed," Elizabeth told the girls. "It'll take them a long time to get through in town and get back here."

The girls reluctantly went back upstairs, but soon were fast asleep. Snowball curled up close to Mandie. It seemed no time before the rooster was crowing and they could hear Morning Star in the kitchen. The girls quickly got dressed and went downstairs. Elizabeth was setting the table.

"I hope they got to town all right." Mandie stretched and yawned. "Those people are awfully mean and rough."

"I'm sure they got there all right. They tied those two with enough rope to wrap around the house," Elizabeth said.

"Eat." Morning Star smiled, pointing to the table.

The girls laughed and at that moment Uncle Wirt came through the door. He glanced around for the men.

"Where are Ned and John?" He looked puzzled.

"Joe and Dimar captured the people who set fire to the barn last night," Mandie said matter-of-factly, "and they've all gone to Bryson City to turn them over to the authorities."

Uncle Wirt stood there listening in amazement while they explained what had happened the night before. He breathed a loud sigh of relief and sat down at the table.

"Not Tsa'ni!" He could hardly believe it.

"Did he ever come home, Uncle Wirt?" Mandie asked.

"No," the old man replied. "Never come home."

Everyone looked at one another, wondering where the boy could have gone. Mandie thought, *He must be ashamed for what he has done and is staying away long enough to get the nerve to face his family.*

Uncle John, Uncle Ned and the boys arrived back from town before they had finished eating and sat down at the table to join them. Joe and Dimar began eating as though they were starving.

"I'm glad you are all back safely," Elizabeth said. "Aren't you going to tell us about your trip?"

"Yes, yes, the law was mighty glad to get our hood-lums. Seems they were wanted in quite a few counties for several different offenses," John related. "Now we can all breathe a sigh of relief."

"We take gold to bank," Uncle Wirt reminded them.

"As soon as we can eat and get it loaded, Uncle Wirt," Uncle John replied.

"Hurry, take away gold," Uncle Ned said.

"Once it's safe in the bank, we'll inform the Chero-kees of its existence," Uncle John stated.

"How do you plan to do that?" Mandie asked.

"Council pow-wow," Uncle Ned told her. "They tell people."

"How will all the people decide what they want to do

with the gold?" she asked.

"They will take a vote. A place will be set up in the council house on the Cherokee reservation," Uncle John explained

Joe finally laid down his fork. "Boy! That sure was good! Now I have the strength to help load that gold."

Uncle Ned rose and took a rifle from the wall. Uncle Wirt examined his own gun, and John picked up his from the the other end of the room.

"Guns?" Elizabeth looked alarmed.

"We need all the protection we can get to get this load in to town. You never know what kind of trouble we might run into," John assured her.

"I know how to use one of those rifles," Joe spoke up. "Can I carry one, too?"

"I do have one more. You and Dimar can decide between you which one will carry it," John said as he reached for the other gun standing by the bed.

Joe took it and then looked at Dimar. "Here, you carry it the first half of the way to town and I'll carry it the second half."

"Fair enough," the Indian boy said, taking the gun.

"Careful, now. The guns are already loaded," John cautioned them.

The girls wanted to help, of course, but were waved aside as the men and boys loaded the gold into the wagon. It didn't take long. Morning Star brought out several quilts to cover the sacks scattered on the floor of the wagon. Joe and Dimar perched on top of them, while the three men climbed onto the driver's seat.

"Please don't be too long. We'll be worried," Elizabeth called to them.

"We'll hurry back," John promised, waving to her.

Then he instructed everyone to keep his gun out of sight. "We don't want to appear too well-armed. It could look mighty suspicious."

Mandie stood watching them pull into the road. Then she lifted her face to the sky. "Please, God, get them there and back safely."

"I trust God to take care of them, too," Sallie said, touching Mandie's shoulder. "I have asked Him into my heart."

"Oh, how wonderful, Sallie!" Mandie hugged her. "Isn't it good to be able to pray and trust God for everything?"

"It sure is, Mandie," she answered, smiling happily.

The men arrived at the bank in Bryson City just as Mr. Frady, the banker, was opening up for the day. He was a short, fat, nervous little man and he jerked around to look at the wagon pulling up at the door. *Three men and two boys—that could mean trouble,* he thought, but then he spotted a familiar face under a wide-brimmed hat.

"John Shaw!" He hurried down the steps to greet him. "It's been a long time!"

"Wilbur, it's good to see you, old man," John returned his greeting. "We are in desperate need of your bank right now." He lowered his voice. "We have about a bushel of gold under these quilts, and we need a safe place to keep it."

Wilbur's gray eyes grew round behind his spectacles. "*A bushel of gold?* Are you joshin' me, John?"

"No, sir, it's real gold," John replied, chuckling at the banker's reaction.

"If I didn't know you, John Shaw, I'd say you had just pulled off a big robbery," Wilbur told him. "Come on in." He opened the door and the two of them stepped inside.

"Let me open the safe before you bring it in," the

banker said, stepping to a large heavy door at the back.

"How about if we drive around to the back door? It won't be so public that way," John suggested.

"Of course. That's the safest way," Wilbur agreed.

They swung the wagon around to the back door and hastily unloaded the gold into the bank's safe. No one was about and Wilbur kept the front door locked until they were finished.

"Now that we have it all in here, tell me, where in the world did it come from and what are you planning to do with it?" Wilbur asked John, as the others returned to the wagon.

"It's very confidential right now, Wilbur, but we'll have it off your hands in a few days. We want to keep it quiet so there won't be a robbery."

Wilbur wiped the sweat from his furrowed brow. "Well, I should hope not! How many people know about it?"

"Just Uncle Ned and Uncle Wirt and the rest of my family—and Dimar, the Indian boy with us," John told him. "I have promised not to discuss our plans right now, but if you do hear anything about a mysterious pile of gold, pretend you never saw it. Is it a deal?"

"You bet!" Wilbur agreed. "But please don't leave it here too long. I would like to sleep at night."

"We'll see you in a few days then," John waved as he left by the back door and joined the others in the wagon.

"Glad job done," Uncle Ned said, with a sigh of relief, as he picked up the reins and they moved through the alley and into the main street.

"Well, it's up to you and Uncle Wirt now to get the word out," John reminded them. "But don't tell anyone where it's being kept."

The two Indians left John and the boys back at Uncle

Ned's cabin and went directly on their mission to tell the Cherokees about the gold.

"Shucks, we didn't even get to use the rifle," Joe complained as he handed the gun back to John inside the cabin.

John hesitated and then said, "Go ahead and try it out. You and Dimar can go back into the woods. You'll find more ammunition in the box over there. Just be careful."

The boys were overjoyed. "Thank you, Uncle John," Joe beamed, taking the rifle back.

"Thank you," Dimar added as the two headed for the door.

Mandie called after them. "You be careful, Joe Woodard, and don't go shooting somebody, you hear?" Joe stopped and turned, laughing at her outburst. "Mandie, you know I have my own rifle at home. This won't be the first time I've used one."

"Yes, but this is a strange place and that's Uncle John's rifle—I know you have never used that one before," the girl answered seriously.

Joe's face turned red as everyone smiled.

"If I didn't like you so much, Amanda Shaw, I'd say something mean!" With that he and Dimar hurried out the door.

Little did Mandie know how close the two boys would come to shooting someone. They walked on through the woods for a while, looking for an appropriate place for target practice. The trees were dense and it was hard to see very far ahead. Then they came to a small clearing.

"How about here?" asked Joe.

"Good," the Indian boy agreed.

Joe shot at a broken limb, and suddenly there was a

loud clanging noise. The boys froze in silence, listening.
Then it came again.

"What's *that*?" Joe whispered.

"Sounds like an animal caught in a trap." Dimar returned the whisper. "Careful, it could be dangerous." He
slowly crept forward, Joe following. The clanging sound
became louder, as if to beckon them on. "I think it's behind that bush over there," Dimar said softly, pointing
ahead.

They cautiously moved toward the bush. Then suddenly they caught a glimpse through the leaves of what
lay on the other side of the bush and they stopped in
shock. There, completely helpless in an abandoned trap,
was Tsa'ni, his foot tightly secured by the metal spring.
He looked at them with a guilty stare as they came into
view. The clanging had stopped.

"Not *you* again!" Joe slapped his hand to his forehead in exasperation.

"It seems all we do is get this boy out of trouble!" Dimar remarked.

"Would you please get this thing off my foot?" Tsa'ni
sounded demanding. "That's all I want you to do."

The boys looked at each other and then at Tsa'ni's
foot. It had been bleeding and was very swollen. Evidently
the boy was in a lot of pain.

Joe stepped aside with Dimar so they could talk.

"I don't see how we can get that thing off his foot,"
Joe whispered. "We don't have tools, and besides, his
foot is all swollen. Let's go for help. He'll think we are just
leaving him alone."

Dimar nodded.

They walked back to Tsa'ni and shook their heads.

"I don't think we can help you. If we turn you loose,

you'll just get into more trouble," Joe said to him. "This way we know where you are."

"You do not deserve any help," Dimar added.

Tsa'ni looked at them in shock. "Please! Just release my foot. I'll get home somehow by myself."

"No, we cannot help you, Tsa'ni," Joe insisted. "We don't have any tools to release that spring."

Joe and Dimar turned and walked away. When Tsa'ni realized they were not going to help him, he called and called after them, "Please! Please!"

Once out of sight, Joe and Dimar started running toward Uncle Ned's cabin. They were almost breathless when they finally got there. Uncle John was chopping wood by the barn and saw the boys coming. He dropped the axe and hurried to meet them.

"Uncle John, we've found Tsa'ni," Joe told him, handing him the rifle. "He's caught in a trap in the woods."

"We told him we would not help him," Dimar said.

"We didn't want him to know we had gone for help. Let him worry a little after all his meanness," Joe added.

"Let me get some tools and we'll go see what we can do," Uncle John said, shaking his head. "He certainly gets into more trouble than anyone I've ever known."

"We'll need a blanket or something to carry him back. His foot is in pretty bad shape, and I don't think he can walk this time," Joe told him, as John went toward the barn for tools.

"Ask Morning Star for one while I get the tools," John replied.

Morning Star got a blanket, some bottles and a cloth from the shelf, and rolled it all up together inside the blanket.

"I go too," she declared. "Special medicine."

Elizabeth understood. "She wants to go with you to doctor him with her medicine. That's what's in the bottles."

Mandie was thinking aloud. "You see, you should never tell a lie. He said he couldn't walk before and it was a lie. Now he really can't walk. I think it happened to him because he lied."

"Yes, he is a bad Cherokee," Sallie agreed.

"You should see his foot. I know he can't walk this time. He must have been caught in the trap ever since we chased him night before last. We lost him in that direction," Joe told them.

"Go." Morning Star went outside to join John as he came from the barn. The boys followed.

It was quite a job prying the trap from Tsa'ni's foot because it was so tightly secured in the swollen flesh. The foot was extremely painful to the touch, but John tried to be careful as he gently but steadily freed the flesh from the prongs of the spring. When the foot was finally free, Morning Star washed it with liquid from one of the bottles. Tsa'ni winced and bit his lip in pain. Then Morning Star gently wrapped it in a clean piece of cloth and stood up.

"Take him," she said, pointing to the boy.

John and the two boys laid Tsa'ni on the blanket and, rolling the edges of it, made a swing to carry him. Since Uncle Ned's house was much closer than Tsa'ni's, they carried him there and laid him on a bed downstairs. Morning Star administered more of her medicine.

"You boys go tell his mother he is here, and when Uncle Ned and Uncle Wirt come back with the wagon, we'll take him home," Uncle John told them. "I'll be outside."

He went out the door, and Joe and Dimar left on their errand.

The two girls had been watching the whole thing from a distance. Tsa'ni had ignored everyone until now and had not spoken a word.

Mandie came over to his bed now. "I'm sorry you are injured, Tsa'ni, but the Bible says you reap what you sow and you sure have sowed some wild lies. I think you had better pray about it. We'll all pray for you."

Tsa'ni looked at her sullenly. "What I do is my business, not yours!"

"You have been messing in our business, Tsa'ni; that's how you got hurt!" she reminded him, standing up and straightening her skirt. "Now that you are really hurt maybe you won't be able to mess in our business anymore."

Elizabeth stepped in. "Amanda, why don't you and Sallie go outside? Let Tsa'ni rest until his grandfather gets back."

"Yes, Mother," Mandie answered as she scooped up Snowball and turned to Sallie. "Come on. We'll see what Uncle John is doing."

Elizabeth did not uphold the things Tsa'ni had done, but she could see how weak he was and she didn't think it was the right time for him to be reprimanded.

Morning Star brought him a bowl of soup, and cradling the boy's head in her lap, she fed him with a spoon. He didn't say a word but greedily swallowed the broth.

Joe and Dimar came back, bringing Tsa'ni's mother with them. She ran to her son, fell to his side and started weeping. Joe and Dimar looked at each other and went back outside.

When Uncle Ned and Uncle Wirt finally came home

with the wagon, John stopped them.

"No use to unhitch the wagon, Uncle Ned," John told them. "We'll be needing it. Uncle Wirt, the boys found Tsa'ni in the woods. He's inside. He has really been hurt this time, I'm afraid."

The two Indians went inside and came back out shortly, carrying Tsa'ni in the blanket. They put him into the wagon, and helped his mother climb in beside him.

"Please hurry back," John said as they pulled away in the wagon. "I want to hear what you've accomplished today concerning the gold."

"Soon," Uncle Ned called back.

As they all sat around Uncle Ned's table later that night, the old man told his news.

"Pow-wow tomorrow, council house," he said. "Told Cherokee Papoose found gold. Cherokee no want gold."

"But you did get all the chiefs to agree to let the Cherokee people vote on what to do with the gold, didn't you, Uncle Ned?" John asked.

"Cherokee vote pow-wow tomorrow, council house," the old man answered.

"You mean you can get all the people together to vote on something that fast?" John asked in amazement.

Uncle Wirt spoke up, "Tell one Cherokee. Cherokee tell another Cherokee. News travel fast."

Mandie smiled at the way he put it. "You mean when you tell one Cherokee something, he will tell another and so on, until they all know?"

Uncle Wirt nodded.

"It sure has been a busy day for the Cherokees," Joe whistled. "Imagine passing the word to over one thousand people in one day!"

"Approximately thirteen hundred to be exact," John

said. "Of course, the families are large in most cases, and they live in large family groups together."

"That's still a lot of people," Mandie agreed.

"So now all the Cherokee people know about the gold?" John asked again.

"Yes, all know," Uncle Ned nodded.

"Did you tell them to come to the council house tomorrow and vote on what they thought should be done with the gold?" John continued. He wanted to be sure they understood each other.

"Yes," Ned said.

Mandie, Sallie and Joe looked at one another.

"Just think, we are the cause of all this," Joe laughed. "I feel kinda good about it when I think of all the good it will do them."

"I'm glad to be a part of it," Sallie said. "I hope the people decide on a good use for the gold."

"Well, I guess we'll know tomorrow," Mandie said, and then turning to Uncle John, she asked, "Can we go over to the council house to watch tomorrow?"

Her uncle hesitated, looking at Ned and Wirt.

"Papoose go. Papoose Cherokee. Papoose vote," Uncle Ned told her.

"You mean I can vote, too, Uncle Ned?" Mandie was excited.

"Mmm," the old man nodded.

"Can I go along for the ride even though I am not Cherokee and can't vote?" Joe asked wistfully.

Uncle Ned and Uncle Wirt both nodded. "Go."

The four youngsters discussed the matter long into the night after they had gone up to bed.

The next day would hold more excitement for them. It would be a day long to be remembered.

Chapter 12 / The Cherokees' Decision

Jerusha, Dimar's mother, came riding up on a pony early the next morning just as Morning Star was putting on the coffee. She walked in through the open doorway, smiling, as she said, "Vote." She put her arms around Mandie, Sallie and Joe and tried to tell them how happy she was that they had found a fortune for the Cherokees.

"Gold," she said, hugging the three. "Find gold. Make Cherokee feel good. People need things."

The three laughed. "Oh, Jerusha, we are so happy for all the Cherokee people. Uncle John says there is enough gold to do a lot of good," Mandie told her. "Maybe you could build a new church, or a hospital, or even a new school."

Jerusha nodded her head. "Vote." Evidently it was a new English word for her and she kept trying it out. She turned to her son and embraced him. "Vote."

"Yes, I will vote," Dimar said, embarrassed by his mother's display of affection.

Morning Star stepped forward. "Sit. Eat." Jerusha sat down and everyone else joined her.

Elizabeth sat next to Dimar's mother. "I'm so glad you could come down to vote. This is such an important thing for the Cherokees. I know you will all agree on something you need."

The woman nodded her head. "We agree what to do with gold."

At that moment more guests arrived. Everyone turned to stare as Tsa'ni was carried into the house by a huge man, who turned out to be his father. His mother, Meli, came in behind them.

"We vote," the man said as he put Tsa'ni on a chair and turned to Uncle Ned. "We vote." Meli took a place at the table.

Uncle John got up from the table and came across the room to shake hands with the man. "Good morning, Jessan. I'm glad to see you."

Jessan replied, "John, long time since we met."

"Where have you been, Jessan?" John asked.

"I take corn to Asheville to sell. Come back to vote," he said.

John turned to Mandie who was listening to their conversation. "This is Jim's daughter, Amanda. Mandie, we call her. Mandie, this is your cousin, Jessan, Uncle Wirt's son."

Mandie got up and smiled at him. "I'm so glad to meet you. I want to get to know all my Cherokee kin-people."

Jessan laughed, showing perfect white teeth. "Lots of Cherokee kinpeople."

"How is Tsa'ni's foot?" she asked.

"Better," Jessan replied. "Well soon."

Mandie liked her cousin, Jessan, immediately. He seemed too nice to have such a miserable son as Tsa'ni.

She was thinking of the many people she would meet when she went with the others to the council house to vote.

Uncle Ned's cabin was practically running over with people, and they soon began loading up for the journey to the council house. Everyone was in a happy mood except Tsa'ni, who never said a word and tried to ignore what the others were saying.

Mandie was glad she didn't have to ride in the same wagon with Tsa'ni. There seemed to be an air of contempt and sulkiness wherever he was. Uncle Wirt and Jerusha rode with him and his parents.

Joe and Dimar sat on either side of Mandie. Joe was aware again of Dimar's interest in Mandie. She never seemed to notice. Joe was determined Mandie would be his wife when they grew up, and he didn't want anyone else making eyes at her. He liked Dimar, but not when he stared at Mandie.

As they arrived at the reservation center the seven-sided, dome-roofed council house came into view. There must have been several hundred Cherokees milling about it. Every Cherokee in North Carolina must have come to vote. They laughed and talked happily with each other. Almost all the women had red kerchiefs tied around their heads. The young girls looked as if they were wearing their best dresses as they shyly chatted with the young Indian men. It seemed to be a great big party.

When Uncle Ned found a place to leave the wagon and unhitch the horses, they all got down and walked to the council house. All the people turned to look at the group. Mandie smiled at them.

Elizabeth turned to Joe. "Well, I guess we're the only white people around, so we'll have to wait outside," she said, laughing. "Let's stand in the shade here by the doorway."

"Sure, Mrs. Shaw," Joe agreed. Turning to Mandie who was going ahead with Uncle John, he called to her. "Don't forget. Vote for a church, a hospital, or a school. Maybe a hospital would be best, the way Tsa'ni keeps getting himself hurt," He laughed.

Mandie called back to him. "Maybe that would be the best anyhow."

She followed the crowd inside. The Indians moved back to make way for her. She gazed at the inside of the huge building. There were bleachers to sit on. Stout log poles held up the dome-shaped thatched roof and the symbols of the clans adorned the posts. The place of the sacred fire was directly ahead as they entered. Behind the fire sat men with stacks of papers and books.

Uncle Ned was watching her, proud to show off his people's council house. He pointed to the men. "Vote," he said and led them across the room. He explained in Cherokee who Mandie was. Most of the Cherokees knew Uncle John from his visits.

The six men sitting behind the papers got up and smiled at her.

"Jim Shaw's papoose vote," one spoke, indicating the papers.

The second man said, "Papoose find Cherokee gold."

Between Uncle John and Uncle Ned they called the men's names as they spoke to the girl, but Mandie was too fascinated with everything to remember who they were. However, she knew they must be important people to occupy the place behind the fire.

The first man handed Mandie a piece of paper. "Vote," he said.

She took the paper, looked at it, saw that it was completely blank, and turned to Uncle John. "What do I do? Just write down what I think should be done with the gold?"

"That's right. Just write down whatever idea you have about using the gold." Uncle John turned to the first man and took a piece of paper for himself. "Have all these people already voted?"

"Yes," the man answered.

"We must be late, Uncle Ned," John whispered to the old man.

Uncle Ned had a sly smile on his face. He moved away from the others and wrote on his piece of paper and handed it back to the man who was giving them out. The man carefully recorded it in his book.

Mandie sat down on a bleacher and wrote the word *hospital* on her slip of paper and returned it to the man, as Uncle John, Morning Star, Dimar and Sallie all gave their papers back to the Indian in charge.

"We wait," Uncle Ned told them, pointing to seats nearby.

Mandie turned and saw Tsa'ni being brought in by his father, Jessan. Meli, Jerusha and Uncle Wirt followed. They took pieces of paper from the men, wrote, and returned them. They turned around and looked at Mandie and her group.

Mandie quickly turned to Dimar and Sallie. "I hope they don't come over here with Tsa'ni."

Before they could reply, the other group headed their way and sat down on the bleachers in front of them. She pulled her long skirt back and moved her feet to keep from touching them. No one spoke. Everyone seemed to be waiting.

The men with the papers began gathering up all their

things. The first one, who had spoken to Mandie, stood up. He beat on a drum a couple of times. Silence fell over the crowd.

"Vote is done. We have counted all votes," he said in a loud, booming voice. "I will read the decision of our people on what to do with the gold found in the cave." He picked up one of the open books and began reading from it. "We, the Eastern Band of Cherokee Indians of North Carolina, do not wish to accept the gold found in the cave." He paused and looked up.

Mandie couldn't believe her ears.

He continued, "Even though it was purported to have belonged to our great warrior Tsali and to be left by him for our people, gold has always brought bad luck to our people. Therefore, we hereby designate as the holder of the gold with complete authority to use it as she wishes, the daughter of our beloved Jim Shaw, who has gone on to the happy hunting ground. We leave it in the hands of Amanda Elizabeth Shaw, who found the gold, to do whatever she deems best with it. Signed—The Eastern Band of Cherokee Indians of North Carolina."

Mandie was really in a daze now. She couldn't even think straight. The gold belonged to her Cherokee kin-people and was worth a fortune, according to Uncle John, but here they were refusing to accept it and were giving it entirely over to her. She didn't know what to do.

The man was still talking. "This decision was made unanimously. There was not a dissenting vote."

Mandie heard that all right. That meant Tsa'ni had voted in her favor also. She just couldn't believe it was happening. She must be dreaming. She pinched herself to see if she was awake.

"Amanda Shaw, would you please come up here and

accept the decision of our people?" He was looking straight at her, waiting.

Mandie turned to Uncle John. "Uncle John, I can't walk up there. I'm too scared. Why did they do such a crazy thing?"

Uncle John smiled, got up and took her hand, pulling her to her feet. "Come on. I'll go with you." He walked over to the man, practically dragging Mandie with him. The man extended the sheet of paper to Mandie.

"This is your authorization from the Cherokee people," he said.

Mandie trembled as she took the paper and turned to face the hundreds of Cherokees. "Oh, I love you, my Cherokee kinpeople. I love you." Tears came into her blue eyes. She held the paper against her heart. "I'll do my best, with Uncle John's and Uncle Ned's and Uncle Wirt's help, to use the gold wisely."

Something that sounded like a war whoop went up from the hundreds of Cherokees as they showed their gratitude. Mandie just stood there, unable to move. The first thing she knew Joe was tugging at her hand.

"Mandie, let's get out of here," he whispered.

The crowd started moving. The people passed by to speak to her, some in English, some in Cherokee.

She lifted her face as she moved along toward the others. "Thank you, God. Thank you. My people do love me."

She and Uncle John sat back down. Joe and her mother had taken seats next to them, now that the voting was over. Everyone was saying nice things to her, but she couldn't understand a thing they were saying. She was still in a daze.

She was staring directly into Tsa'ni's face as he

turned to look at her. He managed to get up on his good foot and extend his hand to her as he turned around.

"Love, my cousin, love!" he said, his face lit up by a big smile. "Please, forgive me!"

"Oh, Tsa'ni, my cousin, love!" She smiled and put her arms around his neck and kissed him on the cheek. "My Cherokee kinpeople."

She turned and smiled at the people surrounding her. "I think we will build a hospital for my people!"

The crowd cheered.

She was sure she had made the right decision.

But now she felt that something even greater had been accomplished. She had gained her cousin's love and acceptance as a Cherokee. God had overruled. After having struggled so long with negative thoughts toward her cousin, the battle was won. She was proud to be part Cherokee, and even prouder to be a Christian.